REX ZERO

THE GREAT PRETENDER

ALSO BY TIM WYNNE-JONES

STORIES

Lord of the Fries and Other Stories

The Book of Changes: Stories

Some of the Kinder Planets

NOVELS

Rex Zero, King of Nothing

Rex Zero and the End of the World

A Thief in the House of Memory

The Boy in the Burning House

Stephen Fair

The Maestro

REX ZERO

THE GREAT PRETENDER

TIM WYNNE-JONES

FARRAR STRAUS GIROUX · NEW YORK

First published by Groundwood Books Limited, Canada
First American edition, 2010
Printed in September 2010 in the United States of America
by RR Donnelley & Sons Company, Harrisonburg, Virginia
Designed by Natalie Zanecchia
10 9 8 7 6 5 4 3 2 1

www.fsgkidsbooks.com

Library of Congress Cataloging-in-Publication Data
Wynne-Jones, Tim.
    Rex Zero, the great pretender / Tim Wynne-Jones.— 1st American ed.
      p. cm.
    Sequel to: Rex Zero, king of nothing
    Summary: In 1963, when his family moves across town to a new
school district in Ottawa, Canada, twelve-year-old Rex conspires with
best friends James, Kathy, and Buster to attend the school in his old
neighborhood.
    ISBN: 978-0-374-36260-7
    [1. Moving, Household—Fiction.   2. Schools—Fiction.
3. Friendship—Fiction.   4. Honesty—Fiction.   5. Family life—Canada—
Fiction.   6. Ottawa (Ont.)—History—20th century—Fiction.
7. Canada—History—1945– —Fiction.]   I. Title.

PZ7.W993Ri 2010
[Fic]—dc22

                                                           2008055569

TO ALL MY BELOVED COMPEERS
AT VERMONT COLLEGE,
ONE AND ALL, OLD AND NEW

OH-OH YES, I'M THE GREAT PRETENDER
PRETENDING THAT I'M DOING WELL . . .

—from "The Great Pretender,"
by the Platters, 1956,
written by Buck Ram

THE GREAT PRETENDER

THE SINISTER SIGN POST

'm sitting on the top step outside my house, my feet firmly planted about a foot apart, my hands out straight in front of me holding tight to the handle of the towline, just the way Buster showed me. Except there isn't really a towline. It's my flashlight. Buster is going to teach me how to water-ski and I want to get in all the practice I can on dry land.

We're going up to his grandmother's cottage in Québec. James is coming, too. Four whole days at Lac Philippe: canoeing, fishing, messing about in boats. It's a dream come true! Last summer when James went up to Buster's, I wished so hard that I'd get invited up there that my wish tank must have filled right to the top and sloshed over into my dream tank. I dreamed of what it would be like and now I'm going to find out firsthand.

I get up, walk down the path, and look west on Clemow Avenue. I can see the Keatons' station wagon in their driveway about ten houses up on the other side of the street. It's a brand-new navy blue 1963 Oldsmobile Dynamic 88. They're filling it up with food and stuff for the cottage. There's Clem now, hefting a big yellow cooler. He's seventeen, Buster's older brother. The cooler looks heavy. It's probably full of Coke and root beer and cream soda and ice cream sandwiches. He goes back inside the house. They've been loading for the last half hour. It's a big car.

I go back and sit on the porch. I'm supposed to wait here. I offered to help but Mr. Keaton has a "system"— that's what he called it. He's a mathematician, so he's probably got it worked out to the last inch. I tighten the strings around my sleeping bag. I open my suitcase for the nth time and check on everything: marshmallows, paper bag full of Mum's peanut butter cookies, large box of Smarties, new Hardy Boys: *The Sinister Sign Post*. It's the fifteenth; I'm reading them in order. There are clothes, too, but not many. I plan to eat, sleep, and swim in my bathing suit!

I walk down to the street again to check on how the packing is going and I see my sister Annie Oakley on her bike tearing around the corner at Lyon Street going about a hundred miles an hour. She's up on her feet, bent low and flying, like she's in a race for her life. She swerves up onto the sidewalk and barrels toward me, full tilt. I jump back onto the lawn as she veers up the path.

"Here," she says, and throws me a baseball, which I

drop because I wasn't expecting it. Then she's back on her bike and hightailing it up our driveway. I hear the clatter of her bike as she drops it, then the back door slam.

It's a hardball, scuffed but pretty new. I look up, and, sure enough, two boys are biking toward me. I can guess whose ball it is. I hide it behind my back, just before the first of them screeches to a stop in front of me. He's Annie's age, about fourteen, with Popeye biceps. He's breathing hard. He stares up at the house.

"Is it this one?" he says to the other guy, who's wearing a Milwaukee Braves cap. Popeye's face is red. Pooped red. Angry red.

Milwaukee nods. And then they look straight at me, their front wheels inching up onto the lawn. I step backward.

"You see a girl come this way?" says Popeye.

I shake my head, which is easy to do because I never really think of Annie as a girl.

"Curly brown hair, scratched-up knees," says Popeye.

"And some stolen property," growls Milwaukee. Then he leans out over his handlebars and looks me hard in the eye. "Hey, you're her brother," he says. I've never seen him before; how did he know that? Do I tell him I didn't *choose* to be her brother?

"Where is she?" says Popeye.

He's giving me the evil eye, all right, and any second now he's going to wonder why my hands are behind my back. Then what? I imagine my arms in casts—how hard it would be to water-ski. So I show Popeye the ball. He grabs it from me.

"There she is," says Milwaukee. He's pointing up toward the second floor of the house. I turn to look, catch a glint of sun on glasses behind a lace curtain.

"No, that's a different one," I say. Letitia is three years older than Annie. She's probably deciding which of these guys she'd like to marry.

"You tell Annie something," says Popeye, shoving the ball in his bike bag. "Tell her this is the last straw. You got it? We catch her and she's dead."

"Even if she stays out of our way all summer, she's *still* dead," says Milwaukee. "Soon as she gets back to school. Bam!"

"Damn right," says Popeye. "She should be locked up."

I nod. I've often thought the same thing.

"Come on," snarls Milwaukee. "Let's get out of here."

"You make sure you tell her, kid," says Popeye.

"I promise," I say. "Sorry about the ball."

Then they're gone. And about two seconds later, the front door opens and Annie steps out onto the porch with a cherry Popsicle in her hand and a cherry grin.

"They're going to kill you," I say. "Why'd you steal their ball?"

"Because Dwayne kicked me."

"You were playing baseball with them?"

"Are you kidding? It was last fall. Dwayne Fontaine."
She makes his name sound like a plumbing problem. She
takes a vicious bite of her Popsicle. "He said it was a mistake," she says, through the cold lump in her mouth. "But I
know he did it on purpose." She glowers at the memory.
"And Bobby Rinaldo hit that ball at me today when he saw
me ride by. Hit it over the fence—right at me!"

"That's called a home run."

"Hah!" she says. "It was deliberate."

I roll my eyes. "Sheesh, Annie."

"Just because I put a cow's eye in his locker, last year."

I stare at her in disbelief. I almost ask what Bobby did
to deserve a cow's eye in his locker, but I don't bother.

"A cow's eye?"

"We were dissecting them in biology. I took a couple
extra."

That's my sister. Always planning ahead.

"What are you going to do?" I ask. "They're going to kill
you."

"They'll never catch me."

"They said they'll get you at school."

"Yeah, well good thing we're moving," she says. And
then immediately her face clouds over. "Oops."

"What did you say?"

"Nothing."

"Moving?"

"Forget it," she says. "I was . . . aw, just forget it." She turns back toward the house and I run after her, catch her by her shirttail in the front hall as she's about to head upstairs.

"What do you mean, moving? We've only been here a year."

"Keep your voice down," she hisses. "We're not supposed to know."

I keep my voice down but it's all shaky. "Where?"

"Not far."

"Last time was three thousand miles, so not far could mean anything."

"Keep your shirt on, Rex. We're just moving across town somewhere."

"But, but—"

I don't get to finish because right then a car honks in front of the house. Three loud beeps. I look out the window. It's the Keatons.

"Have a great time," says Annie, waving her Popsicle. Then she dashes upstairs leaving drips like blood on every step.

THE ONE THAT GOT AWAY

Moving. I try to put it out of my mind. Swinging on a fat rope out over the lake, I forget about moving. Water-skiing, I forget about moving. Eating hot dogs roasted on a stick over a fire on the beach, I forget about moving. I hook the biggest largemouth bass in the world and I'm not thinking about moving one bit. Then suddenly the bass leaps, all shiny in the sun, spits my worm out of his large mouth, and dives down into the dark green water. Gone.

At night, playing board games by a kerosene lamp or sitting on the screened-in porch, while Buster's brother Clem plays Everly Brothers' songs on his guitar, I almost forget about moving completely. I sing the harmony to "Wake Up Little Susie" and Clem says I've got a good voice.

Then it gets quiet and I remember what Annie said and I don't want to sing anymore.

James says, "What's eating you, Rex?" And I just shrug.

Saturday it's so hot Buster, James, and I sleep out on the porch. We lie there listening to the crickets and the frogs, the moths banging against the screen, the mosquitoes singing "Wee-oo, wee-oo, let me in wee-oo." There's a splash out on the lake.

"Bet that's the one that got away," says Buster. "Boy did he move."

There it is again. Moving. Annie could be wrong. She gets most everything wrong. She jumps to conclusions all the time and the conclusions don't like it one bit. So why am I so sure she's right?

"Hopewell is going to be great," says James.

"Don't talk about school," says Buster. "It's bad luck."

"Yeah," I say.

"But it's a good name for a school," says James.

I don't say anything. Hopewell Avenue is the new school we're going to in September for grade seven. Where we're supposed to go, all three of us.

"I guess there isn't any other way to hope except well," says James.

"Huh?" says Buster.

"Hope*well*," says James. "You can't hope badly, can you? It kind of defeats the purpose."

"Oh, right," says Buster.

I swallow hard. "Yeah, but you can hope against hope," I say.

"I've never understood that expression," says Buster.

"Like two boxers," says James. Then he puts on a voice like a ring announcer. "In this corner wearing yellow trunks, you've got Hope; in the other corner, in black trunks, you've got Hope."

"Which is good," says Buster. "Because that way Hope can't lose."

"I hope not," I say.

◎ ◎ ◎

When I get home Sunday afternoon, the house is empty. Maybe my family already moved. Great. I've got my sleeping bag. I'll just settle down right here.

In the almost silence, I notice the record player is on. The needle is at the end of an album going around and around: thwicka, thwicka, thwicka, with no song left to play. It's *Harry Belafonte, Live in Concert at Carnegie Hall.* Mum must be here somewhere.

I find her in the basement in the House of Punch. There's a big mahogany table in the center of the dusty old room. Annie took all of these fat hardbound volumes of *Punch* magazines off the shelves and piled them up around the table to make an air-raid shelter last fall when the world was about to end. Mum doesn't even notice me at the door. She's sitting on the table with one of the volumes open on her lap. She's already put several of the volumes back on the shelf. She smiles at some cartoon and turns the page. One arm rests across her stomach. She squeezes it and a sour look creeps across her face as if she's got an ache.

I clear my throat and she looks up. "Oh, hello, Rex. Did you have a good time?"

I nod. I want to tell her about all the things we did, the giant fish I almost caught. But those aren't the words that come out. "Are we moving again, Mum?"

She folds her hands together on the open book. She looks down at her hands and I know we are.

She sighs. "We're only renting this house, Rex. You knew that."

"Yes, but the owner lives in the Far East or somewhere."

"The South Pacific."

"So?"

"So, he's decided to move his family back here."

"It isn't fair."

Mum stares down at her hands again. She turns her wedding ring around and around.

"I know what you mean," she says, "but actually the owner is being quite fair. We only had a yearlong lease and he's giving us the rest of the summer to find a new home."

To find a new home. I slide down the doorframe until I'm sitting on the faded, threadbare Oriental carpet that covers the floor. I can feel the chill of the concrete through it, smell the dampness, the mildew.

"I thought finally we were going to *stay* somewhere for once."

"I know."

I pound the carpet and dust puffs up. "When we move it will be the eighth house I've lived in. The eighth! I'm twelve years old and I've lived in eight houses."

"Rex, what can I say? Do you really think I want to move?"

I glance up at her and then down at the carpet. A lot of words pile up in my mouth: words with spikes and claws and sharp teeth. "It isn't fair," I say finally, pounding my hand on the carpet again. "It just isn't—"

"Rex," says Mum, and her voice snaps like a whip, so that all the angry animals waiting to leap out of my mouth scurry back down my throat. "Rex," she says again, her voice softer—a little, anyway.

There's only one grimy window into this room and one bare bulb just above her head. Its light falls more on her hands and the open pages of the book than on her face, but I can see how hard she's trying to keep her face smooth, her eyes still. "Rex," she says a third time, her voice sad.

"For the first twenty-one years of my life I lived in one house," she says. "One lovely, happy house. Then I married your father." She pauses, crosses her arms. "Do you have any idea how much work it is to move a family of eight even if it is only a few miles?"

I want to say that there are only seven of us now that Cassie is married, but then what she just said registers.

"Just a few miles?"

She nods.

"So I'll be able to go to Hopewell?"

"I'm afraid not," she says. "We looked in the Glebe—believe me—and in Ottawa South. I love it here. But there was nothing affordable nearby. Nothing large enough. We have, however, found a wonderful big house in the west end." She frowns. "Well, your father thinks it's wonderful. I'm inclined to see it as just plain big, since I will be the one doing the cleaning."

"Where's the west end?"

"Where do you think?"

"I mean, is it far?"

Mum shakes her head, but she's not answering my question; she's shaking it off. She's fed up with my whiny voice and so am I, but it's the only voice I have handy. I left my nice voice up at the cottage, I guess; the voice that asked politely for a second hamburger and more relish. She sighs again.

"It's a fine neighborhood, Rex. Lots of trees. Apparently, the front lawn is a blaze of lilies of the valley in the spring. That should be nice." She takes a deep breath as if she's sniffing those lilies. Then she lets it out and just looks tired. "Anyway, I'm sure there will be a perfectly good school for you," she says. "And I will be the one to register you in it. And find a primary school for Flora Bella and register her. And register Letitia and Annie in high school, although I suppose they're old enough to do it themselves by now—though one can never tell with Annie. Then I'll find out where to shop for groceries and where the dry cleaner is, to get your father's shirts starched the way he likes them, and arrange for the milk delivery and the newspaper, the water to be turned on and the oil to be delivered for the furnace, so that we don't freeze to death, and the electricity, so you don't have to do your homework in the dark and—"

"Okay, I get it, Mum."

"Thank you," she says.

Now we're both mad and I'm not sure whose move it is. Mum sighs, shuts the book on her lap, gets up, and places it on the shelf. I watch her grip the shelf for a moment after she has put the book down. Some kind of cramp, I guess. It passes. She runs her hand down the back of the volume in front of her. "My father used to read *Punch*," she says. "Do you remember your grandfather?"

I try to think. "Is he dead?"

Her shoulders droop. "No, he's *not* dead."

"Sorry. I couldn't remember."

"No. How could you? You haven't seen him since you were three." She turns to me. "He's not dead, Rex, but he's a long way away. And I miss him so much. Him and Mum."

I hope she isn't going to ask me to write to them. She does that sometimes, but I never can think of what to say because I don't know them.

"Maybe you could help put these books away," she says.

I want to say that Annie was the one who took them down, but before I can say anything, she places her hand over her mouth and starts heading for the door. I move my legs out of her way as she charges past and up the stairs to the kitchen. I hear her feet in the hallway overhead, a door open and shut: the downstairs bathroom. Then I hear the unmistakable sound of someone throwing up. I guess she really doesn't like moving, either.

HOPE WELL

We bike out to the new house: Kathy, James, Buster, and I. It only takes about thirty-five minutes, but the last bit is up a steep hill so we arrive out of breath and dripping sweat. I've been there already so I know what to expect.

"It's huge," says Buster.

"And yellow," says Kathy.

"Dirty yellow," I say.

There's a three-foot-high stone retaining wall across the front of the property, where we rest our feet. The mortar is ancient and crumbly, like maybe the Romans built it. We sit there on our bikes staring through the trees and the scruffy shrubbery at the yellow monster. There are three steps up from the sidewalk to a path, which is cracked and weedy. There's a bunch more steps halfway up the front lawn and then stone stairs up to a wide porch, deep in shadows, with four ugly square pillars holding up an enclosed patio all across the second floor. The front door is brown. Everything else is dirty yellow brick, peeling yellow wood—the color of the old newspapers Mum stores potatoes in down in the basement.

There's a dormer window at the top.

Buster cranes his neck and shields his eyes. "Is that your room up there?" he asks.

I shake my head. "Annie claimed it. I get the back room in the attic."

Buster laughs. "I wouldn't have wanted to be around when your folks told *her* you were moving," he says.

"She's glad," I say. "There are two guys at her old school who want to kill her."

"Only two?" says James.

"What about your other sisters?" asks Kathy. "And your little brother?"

I pound my foot on the crumbly wall and dislodge some mortar. "No one cares. Flora Bella is excited about getting a huge bedroom, which Mum says they'll paint pink. Letitia is all excited about Fisher Park High School because Paul Anka used to go there."

"Really? The guy who wrote 'Diana' and 'Puppy Love' and 'The Teen Commandments'?"

"Really. Also, her voice teacher lives about three blocks away, so she's over the moon. And the Sausage doesn't care where we live since he doesn't have any friends—probably because he cries all the time."

We lean our bikes against the wall and head up the

path. There's no sign of any lilies of the valley on the lawn but the grass is so high it would be hard to see them anyway. There are straggly bushes everywhere and maple trees and a huge beech tree, so it's shady and ten degrees cooler than out on the street. We walk around the side of the house to the backyard. It's big and shady, too, and there's a round fishpond in the middle surrounded by a stone wall.

We lean over and look down. The water's low and brown and clogged with dead leaves. A frog's snout sticks out. Then he sees us, I guess, because he dives under cover again.

No one has cut the grass in about a hundred years. The shrubbery looks like it just went through electric shock therapy. There is another wall at the back end of the garden, overgrown with ivy. It's about chest-high. We all look over it, down onto Gwynne Street, which is lower than the garden.

"Good place for pouring oil on the invaders," says James.

"Stop trying to cheer me up," I say.

"Hey, look at this," says Buster. He's found the shed in the northwest corner of the garden. It's got a low roof of slate tiles covered with moss. "Crazy, man," he says, peering through the window, which is smeared with grime and straggly cobwebs. I push open the door, which screeches like a horror movie, and we duck inside. There's an old bench under the window littered with broken flowerpots, dead flies, and mouse poop. There's a stack of tin buckets against the wall filled with nuts and bolts and hinges and dust-covered bits of wire. A worn-out broom leans against the wall, next to a rusty lawn mower, a wheelbarrow, and gunnysacks filled with who knows what. Dead people, by the look if it. I sniff. Could be.

"This is excellent," says James.

"I know. I asked Mum and Dad if I could clean it up and move in here."

"Perfect," says Buster.

"Dad said I could as long as I fumigated myself every time I set foot in the house."

Buster stamps his foot on the floor. "Maybe there's a secret underground room," he says.

"Like in *The Disappearing Floor*," says James.

"Shhhh!" I say, covering my ears. *The Disappearing Floor* is number nineteen of the Hardy Boys books. I'm only at *The Twisted Claw*.

We head out into the yard again and I pull the door shut. I have to yank pretty hard and the hinges scream in protest.

Out front again, I sit on the retaining wall, my Keds dangling above the sidewalk. Kathy is on one side of me, James on the other. Buster goes over to look at the flagpole. Dad says the house used to be an embassy. Buster stares up the pole as if maybe there might still be a tattered flag up there lost amid the branches of the beech tree.

"It's a pretty neat place," says Kathy.

"Yeah," says James. "We'll come out to visit lots."

"Thanks," I say, but I know I don't sound very thankful.

Nobody says anything for a moment or two. Buster wanders off, back to the shed, I bet, to see if there really is a secret underground room. What I need is a secret underground *passage* that leads all the way to Hopewell Avenue School.

I grab a hank of weeds, yank them out of the ground, and throw them on the sidewalk.

Kathy touches my arm. "We'll get together every weekend, Rex," she says.

I snatch my arm away. "I don't want to get together every weekend. I want to get together *every day*." They don't say anything and I don't say what I'm really thinking, which is that we won't get together every weekend, no matter what Kathy thinks. I've moved eight times and I know. Things will come up. Best friends find other best friends—new best friends. Soon they forget what you look like, forget your name. They don't even write.

"It's not so far by bus," says Kathy.

I don't answer.

"My mom used to work at the Civic Hospital which is three or four blocks thataway," she says, pointing west. "She'd take the number six every day and get there in about ten or fifteen minutes."

"Really?"

She nods. "From the Glebe. Hardly any time at all."

"Hmmm . . ."

"What are you thinking?" says James.

"Ten or fifteen minutes?" I say to Kathy.

She nods. "From Bank all the way to Holland."

"The number two on Bank Street goes all the way to Hopewell, right?"

Kathy nods again. James nods, too.

"So you could probably transfer from the six to the two?"

Kathy's eyes get wider and wider. "Are you thinking what I'm thinking?" she says.

"I don't know. What are you thinking?"

Buster arrives back and plunks himself down on the wall.

"Who's thinking what about what?" he asks.

"Rex is thinking maybe he could go to Hopewell, after all," says Kathy. "Am I right?"

There! Somebody else said it. It isn't just me being crazy. "Yeah," I say. "Why not?"

"Because you can't," says Buster. "You have to go to the school that you have to go to."

"Why?"

"Because you have to. It's probably the law. Anyway, they know you're coming to live out here and if you don't show up at your proper school they'd send a truant officer to get you."

"Proper school?" I ask. "What school? How could they know I'm coming when we haven't even moved yet?"

"Yeah, but the Board of Education knows."

"This isn't Russia," says Kathy. "In Russia maybe they

know what everybody's doing, but over here nobody knows anything."

"She's right," says James. "I think the way it works is that our old school sent transcripts over to Hopewell for each student. So unless one of your parents de-registered you, you're probably still on the class list there."

I don't know how these things work. Then I remember what Mum said about having to register me at my new school, which must have meant she hadn't done it yet. And I remember something else she said—something even better.

"Holy garbanzos."

"What?"

So I tell them about what Mum said about my sisters registering themselves at the high school. "Maybe I could register myself at the new school—*or pretend to*. Why not?"

"Great!" says James.

"Do it!" says Kathy. She grabs my arm so tightly it hurts. But it's a good hurt—the kind of hurt that makes you realize you're alive.

Buster just rubs his flattop. "I've got a bad, bad feeling about this."

TICK MARKS IN THE GOOD COLUMN

My mind is buzzing and bouncing around like a bee in a flower shop. I'm glad I have such smart friends. James is the one who figures out we should find the school I'm supposed to go to while we're out here, so that when the time comes I can pretend to register there.

Kathy is the one who figures out that I should probably go out to Hopewell sometime soon and make sure they got my transcripts from Mutchmor. That's where we went last year. "Make sure they're expecting you," she says.

But Buster is the one who figures out the most important thing of all. "You're going to have to lie to your parents," he says.

I was trying not to think of that. "Maybe I won't have to lie. If I figure it all out and I can get to school on time by bus and everything, maybe they won't mind me going to Hopewell."

"But you'll still have to lie to the Board of Education," says Buster. "You'll be a criminal."

"Since when is it criminal to go to school?" says Kathy.

"There's another little problem," says James. "Moolah."

"Moolah?"

"Bus tickets."

Oh, right.

"They're four for a quarter," says Buster. "That's ten tickets a week, which means sixty-two and a half cents per week."

How does he do that?

"What's your allowance, Rex?"

He knows what my allowance is: twenty-five cents per week.

"Moolah-schmoolah," says Kathy. "Let's go find your new *not* school."

So we ride down Fairmont with no idea where we're going, except that the road is steep and we have to keep our brakes on the whole way down. There are trees, like Mum said, but they don't make an archway over the road like on Clemow. There's a park and we find some kids about our age and ask them where the intermediate-level school is.

"Connaught," says one guy, and points down Fairmont. "Turn left at Gladstone."

We ride on until we get to Gladstone, turn west, and a few blocks later, there it is.

We bike past it, slowly. And then bike past it again. It looks just like a school, a big heap of brown bricks and windows full of darkness and sky. We reconnoiter the joint, like robbers before a break-in.

"That's probably the office," says Kathy, pointing at some windows on the first floor. "That's where you'll have to *not* go to register." She laughs, but now the reality of this caper hits me: how am I ever going to pull it off?

"How *do* you register?" I ask.

"Don't sweat it," says Kathy. "You're not registering, remember? That's the point."

"Yeah, but your parents are going to want some proof that you did," says Buster. "How are you going to do that?"

I've never thought about any of this stuff before. As far as I know you just show up at school the day after Labor Day and they have a place for you. I scratch my head. James is scratching his head as well. He has this gray patch about the size of a quarter as if he started getting wise right from birth.

"There's probably something to fill out with your address and phone number and all that."

"Yeah," says Buster, "and your dad or mum will have to sign it."

"You could probably forge your dad's signature," says Kathy.

"And then you will *really* be breaking the law," says Buster.

We think some more. Kathy twists her long blond hair

into a rope and bites on it. She looks like she's ready to plow Buster in the kisser.

"Or," says James, but he doesn't say any more, because he's still thinking—you can see it in his eyes.

"Or what?" says Buster.

"Or you could bring back the registration stuff for your parents to sign and then offer to take it back to the school for them, and—"

"Sort of happen to lose it!" says Kathy. "Brilliant!"

Buster groans. "This just gets worse and worse."

◎ ◎ ◎

August comes and my birthday. My twelfth birthday. We go bowling at King Pin—forty balls for a dollar. We make teams: Kathy, James, and Sami Karami against Buster, Polly Goldstein, and me. It's strange having Polly there because I only really know her from school. But I ran into her one afternoon down near the St. James tennis courts on Third. She was all in tennis whites: white sneakers with white laces, white socks, white short skirt, white sweater. Her black hair was pulled back in a ponytail with a white terrycloth bow to hold it in place, and before I knew what was happening I asked her to come to my party.

She's a good bowler.

It's fun, until we get back to my place and have to make our way to the dining room through stacks of boxes. Boxes everywhere.

"You're moving?" says Polly. She looks hurt and I get a lump in my throat.

"Don't worry," whispers Kathy. "He's still going to Hopewell. Right, Rex?"

I nod at her. I nod at Polly—like one of those springy-necked dogs people have in the back window of their car. Then Mum comes in with cake and ice cream and we sit down. Buster glares at me, humming the theme song from *Dragnet*.

"Dum-da-dum-dum. Dum-da-dum-dum-DUH!"

◎ ◎ ◎

I'm going to need bus money. I offer to help pack and clean up and Mum looks pleased until I ask if she can pay me.

"Oh, Lord love a duck," she says. "Do you think anyone is paying me to do all this work?"

I decide I'd better act very mature, very quickly. "I don't really need any money," I say. "I know there's lots to do. Just point me in the right direction."

So she gives me a job to do and I go do it. And then another, and another, and now I have work to do just about every day: little things mostly—errands and stuff. It's okay. I might not be making any money but every job I do is a tick mark in the good column, right?

Clear the dishes—*Tick!* Run to the store to pick up some more Mr. Clean—*Tick!* Take my little brother to the park to keep him out of my mother's hair—*Tick!*

I don't ask for money, but I start looking for it everywhere and I get lucky. I find a dollar and twenty cents' worth of change down the sides of Dad's big chair. I find another thirty cents in telephone booths on Bank Street, and make forty-six cents returning pop bottles I find on the street and in the park. You get two cents a bottle. Mr. Papazian at the Clemow Smoke Shop says I should clean them up a bit first. I guess he means the ones I found in the pollywog pond.

Near the end of August, I bike down to Hopewell, like Kathy suggested. We all met at Mutchmor Public School, but it only goes up to grade six. So I've never set foot in Hopewell and I'm pretty nervous. The teachers aren't around but the doors are open and the secretaries are back at work. I stand in the hallway, outside the office, soaking it all in. *This* is my new school. It smells of disinfectant and wax. I look around and it looks just the way it should look. It looks like the place where I belong.

I take a deep breath and open the office door.

"How might I help you?" says a cheery-looking older woman sitting at a desk behind the counter.

"Hi," I say. "I'm just starting at Hopewell and I wanted to make sure I was registered."

For some reason this makes the woman chuckle. The nameplate on her desk reads Mrs. Swallow.

"Well, isn't that something?" says a younger secretary named Miss Kirkby, looking up from her typewriter. "A real keener."

Mrs. Swallow finds a thick pad of paper on her desk and then comes over to the counter. "What's your name, young man?"

"Rex Norton-Norton," I say. Then I spell it, which makes both the secretaries laugh again. They're so jolly.

"At 197 Clemow Avenue?" Mrs. Swallow asks.

"That's right, ma'am," I say. And it's not even a lie, either. We aren't moving for three days.

"Well, you are registered, all right. And Rex, I can even tell you your homeroom teacher. Would you like to know that?"

I nod, holding my breath.

"It's Mrs. Beauregard," she says. She shows me my name on the list and I see Kathy, James, Buster—and even Polly—are on it, too. We're all going to be in the same class.

"Mrs. Beauregard has been with us forever."

Miss Kirkby chuckles.

Forever. I like the sound of that.

"Thank you," I say.

◎ ◎ ◎

I check out the buses, too. I feel like one of those thieves in a bank heist movie where every detail has to be timed. I lock up my bike at Fairmont Avenue and head off, pretending it's a normal school day. It takes me forty minutes to get to Hopewell.

"It might be different first thing in the morning," says James.

"Yeah, with rush hour," says Buster. "It might take you two years."

"Don't be stupid," says Kathy.

"I meant two years in the pen," says Buster.

◎ ◎ ◎

Saturday, August 24, 1963. Moving day. Overcast. Rain on the way. My oldest sister, Cassiopeia, comes to help with her new husband, Brian: Mr. and Mrs. Odsburg. She's a lot nicer now that she doesn't live with us anymore. The moving company men do all the heavy lifting, but everyone pitches in, even the Sausage. He carries his teddy bear to the nursery. All Letitia does is get the moving men drinks of lemonade. Annie wants to help unload the van.

"Whoa, watch it there, little lady," says one of the movers.

Annie glares at him and hoists a dresser. "I am *not* a lady," she says, and manhandles the dresser down the ramp. That mover had better watch his step.

I pitch in more than anyone.

"Where does this go?" I say. "And this? And this? And this?" Until Mum pleads with me: "Stop, Rex! Please!" So I say, "Okay, no problem," and I run up to the attic, to my new room, and put it all together just the way I want it. I hang up things and put things on my shelves. I organize my books in alphabetical order. I put my clothes away and then carry all the empty cardboard boxes downstairs. *Tick!*

"By the shed, old chum," says Dad.

"Where's Mum?" I ask. Wanting her to be impressed.

"She's resting."

Back in my room I lean on my windowsill and look down at the backyard. The lawn is mowed. Who do you think did that? *Tick!*

I rest my chin on my arms. Cassie and Brian gave us a wrought-iron bench for the garden as a housewarming present. They're sitting on it now, beside the fishpond. Too bad it's filled with muck. Funny how different things look from so high up. Mr. Odsburg is going bald. I never knew that before.

I look proudly at my new room. It still smells a bit of fresh paint—periwinkle blue—but other than that it's okay. I'm tired but I feel pretty good. I go and find sheets and pillowcases and make my bed. *Tick!*

Finally, there's nothing else to do, so I dig out the piggy bank that I've been keeping my bus money in. I've been trying not to spend my allowance on candy and comics. I lay out all the change on my bedspread. Six dollars and thirty-three cents. That should be enough to get me into November. Maybe I can get a job delivering newspapers or something.

There's a knock on my door. I hide the piggy bank and the money under my pillow. "Come in."

It's Mum. She smiles when she sees my room. "My goodness, Rex. This is truly astounding!"

"Just trying to help," I say.

She gives me a big hug. She squeezes too tight and I struggle a bit until she lets go.

"Sorry," she says. "I'm just so impressed with how you've come around. I know it hasn't been easy." She smoothes my hair with a wet finger and heads for the door.

"Mum?"

She turns.

"If you want, I could go down to my new school on Monday and get the registration papers."

"Oh, my goodness," she says again, raising her hands to her forehead. "I'd almost forgotten. Would you?"

"Sure. I already know where it is."

"You are a dear," she says. And blows me a kiss before closing the door lightly behind her.

I sit on my bed. That wasn't so bad. I only feel a little queasy.

TOO GOOD TO BE TRUE

The secretary at Connaught doesn't want to give me the forms at first.

"This is awfully late," she says grumpily. "School starts in less than a week."

"We just moved," I say.

"Your parents should really come in."

"Oh. Okay." I turn to go. But "should really" isn't the same as "have to." So I turn back again. "It's just that my dad's away on business and my mum is sort of busy. You know, with my baby brother and all."

Her face softens.

"Well, it's a little irregular," she says, then she gets the forms anyway and puts them in a nice big white envelope with the school's address in the upper left-hand corner.

As I ride home, I try to tote up how many lies I had to tell. I imagine that every lie is a crow with glossy feathers sitting on the bare branches of a leafless old tree.

Then I find some money on the sidewalk. Thirty-three cents. I look around to see if anyone is there, because I don't want to steal the money, even though I need it.

But no one's around. That's a sign, right? A good sign?

Mum is so thankful. "I don't know where I'd have found time to do this," she says, filling in the forms at lunch. She gives me this huge smile. "You really are turning out to be such a wonderful young man." I look at my wieners and beans. I'm afraid to try and swallow another mouthful.

I bike back to the school, right after lunch. *Toward* the school, that is. I have to keep the brakes on all the way down the first block of Fairmont, and I'm not exactly sure where the heck I'm going. I mean, I know where the school is but . . .

I guess I could have at least tried to ask my parents if I could go to Hopewell, but there never seemed to be the right moment. And anyway, if I had asked them and they'd said no and then I went anyway, that would be worse, wouldn't it?

I cross Sherwood. That's the big street at the bottom of our hill. The street flattens out, but it feels as if I'm pedaling uphill anyway. It must be that nice crisp, clean envelope lying in my bike bag: it might as well be an anvil. What am I supposed to do with it? I can hear Buster humming in my brain: "Dum-da-dum-dum. Dum-da-dum-dum-DUHHHHH!"

"Are you all right?"

I've come to a complete stop. I look up and a lady is standing there. She just carried her trash can out to the curb. She's staring at me with a concerned look on her face. I look down the street and everyone's trash cans are out on the curb. Another sign.

I cycle on past a few more houses, pull out the registration form, and shove it deep into a trash can. Then I take off, as if I just pulled the pin on a hand grenade and I've got to get as far away as I can.

I ride until I come to the Ottawa River. I'm not even sure how I got here. I stare out across the river. The water is wide, dark. I watch a stretch where the water swirls. A whirlpool.

It's done. The deed is done. And a flock of crows lands on the dead tree in my head, cawing their heads off.

◎ ◎ ◎

The hideous sun demon throws open the door of the house. He looks like an iguana on two legs with gray trousers and a thin black belt.

"That's some allergy," says James, handing me the popcorn.

"I guess it's the combination of drinking too much booze and a megadose of weird radiation," I say.

"Wasn't this called something else last time we saw it?" says Buster.

"*Terror from the Sun,*" says James. "Oh, here's the part where he hides in the little girl's playhouse."

Buster takes the popcorn from me. "I don't know why he keeps going outside when he knows the sun is going to turn him into a monster. It's stupid."

It's Friday and we're at Buster's place watching *Shock Theatre* with the first week of Hopewell under our belts. The amazing thing—way more amazing than *The Hideous Sun Demon*—is that I'm here.

I'm not in jail. Everything is okay. In fact, it's more than okay: everything is great. I did it!

The music swells. It looks like Dr. Gilbert McKenna is going to go out in the sun *again*. For an atomic scientist he sure is dumb. But I don't care. We could watch *Pollyanna* and I would be happy. This is what it's all about. Me and my friends. I remember that I used to think if life was a game how come I never got to roll the dice? Well, I just rolled the dice and got lucky seven!

The movie ends. Next week it's *Attack of the 50 Foot Woman*—one of our favorites. And we'll get together to watch it. At Buster's or maybe even at my place. Who knows?

"Don't you love Hopewell?" I say.

"Huh?" says Buster.

"It's such a great school. The best school ever."

Buster shrugs. "I'm not sure about Mrs. Beauregard."

"She's just old," I say.

"I don't know." Buster shakes his head. "I think she could be trouble. Remember Miss Garr?"

"Miss Garr was mental," I say. "Mrs. Beauregard is just . . . old . . . and hard of hearing and—"

"Snippy," says James.

"Snippy? She's not snippy."

"Well, not to *you*," says Buster.

"What's that supposed to mean?"

Buster shrugs. James fidgets.

"You're kind of acting like the teacher's pet," he says.

"What do you mean?"

"Opening the blinds and closing the blinds," says Buster. "Volunteering to be blackboard monitor. Answering questions."

"What's wrong with answering questions?"

"Nothing, as long as you don't answer *all* the questions."

James nods.

"I'm just . . . I don't know. I'm just so happy to be there, I guess."

James makes a face. "Yeah, well, it looks like a pretty good impersonation of a teacher's pet."

Buster jumps up from the couch. "Anyone feel like an Orange Crush?"

"I don't *feel* like one but I'd *like* one," James and I say in unison.

Buster runs upstairs to the kitchen. There's nothing good on the TV. James turns it off. We just sit there.

"Am I really that bad?" I ask.

James crosses his arms and looks down. "Haven't you noticed the groans?"

"Yeah, a little, but—"

"And that guy throwing an eraser at you?"

"Yeah. What a jerk . . ." I can feel the pain of it in my back all over again. I can't think of anything else to say.

"Rex, it's just that you know how to talk to adults. Some kids hate that."

"That's just because I have to meet new adults all the time because we move so much."

"I know," says James quietly. "But this is grade seven, Rex. Don't try so hard."

Buster arrives back with the pop and we can't help talking about our new school, even though it is Friday night. Buster and James think the gym teacher is a little bit creepy. He just seems rugged to me. They think that shop class is sort of cool, but the glue pot stinks and it's a little scary being around so many dangerous tools with guys we don't know too well. Some of them already have hair on their face.

"Stew Lessieur," says Buster, and shudders.

"Was he the one who held that guy's hand down on the belt sander?"

They nod. "And he's the one who threw the eraser at you," says James.

"Oh." I hadn't known that. "Still, it's pretty amazing: all of us in the same homeroom and Sami and Kathy and . . ." I want to add Polly's name to the list, but I keep it to myself.

"You're right, Rex," says James. "It's pretty good. Especially music."

"Oh, God!" says Buster, throwing himself back on the couch and kicking his feet in the air. "Miss Hotchkiss," he shouts. "I am going to marry her."

"Not if I marry her first," says James.

"Sorry, guys," I say. "I already asked her."

"Maybe we could all marry her," says James.

"That would be bigamy," says Buster.

"No, trigamy," says James.

The truth is Miss Hotchkiss is the most beautiful teacher in the history of music.

"Miss KissKiss," says James.

Buster hugs a big gold cushion. "I think she looks like Liz Taylor but with a pointier chin."

"No way," says James. "She looks like Ava Gardner but with smaller . . . you know."

We laugh Orange Crush laughs.

"Where will we go on our honeymoon?" asks James.

"Hawaii," says Buster. Then he gasps. "Imagine Miss KissKiss in a bathing suit!"

The room is suddenly silent as we all imagine Miss Hotchkiss in a bathing suit. I see her in an itsy-bitsy yellow bikini with little blue treble clefs and notes and rests all over it.

"I've already thought of what I'm going to do for our big music project," I say. It just bursts out of me.

Buster puts down the cushion he's been smooching. He scrunches up his nose. "What?"

"A piano," I say. "I'm going to make a piano."

"The project isn't due until the end of October," says James.

"I know, but I was thinking I'd get a head start."

"A piano?" says Buster.

"Just a small one," I say. I hold up my hands to show them what I mean: a miniature piano. But they're giving me this strange look like I've been out in the sun too long and I'm turning into an iguana, like poor old Dr. Gilbert McKenna in *The Hideous Sun Demon*.

"What's so bad about wanting to do a project early instead of waiting until the last minute?"

Buster shakes his head. "What's gotten into you?"

"Nothing."

"You're acting really sucky," says James.

". . . I just don't want to take any chances," I say. "You know."

Buster groans and rolls his eyes. He pulls the cushion over his face. But James looks me straight in the eye.

"What you *don't* want to do is draw attention to yourself," he says. "If you suck up too much, that's when people get suspicious, right?"

I hadn't thought of that.

"Listen," says Buster. "That guy who threw the eraser at you, Stew Lessieur: Donnie was telling me about him. He's a hockey star. He's our age but he plays hockey with sixteen-year-olds."

"What's that got to do with anything?"

"He doesn't like you."

"Hey, just because he threw an eraser at me—"

Buster makes a noise like some space monster about to heave. "I sit beside him, Rex. Stew Lessieur thinks you're an idiot."

"Oh."

The room gets quiet. I look at James. He nods. "He's the kind of guy you really *don't* want noticing you."

"Why didn't you tell me this before?"

James scratches his head. "We tried."

"Rex," says Buster. "The last thing you need, considering your situation, is an enemy. Someone who might turn you in."

"That's crazy. Nobody's going to turn me in."

"Then just play it cooly-cool, boy," says Buster. "Okay?"

I look down at the empty popcorn bowl. There are a few kernels left, the ones that didn't get popped. They just lie there in the bottom of the bowl, all salty and hard. I nod, but I don't look up.

A KNUCKLE FULL OF NICKELS

H ow come you don't ride your bike to school?" says Annie.

We're sitting at the breakfast table. Flora Bella is smearing lemon curd on an English muffin, pushing it into the holes with her finger. Letitia is outside in the garden looking after the Sausage. Or she's supposed to be. I can hear her singing. The Sausage has probably drowned by now in the fishpond. Mum is cutting up stuff at the counter. And Annie is glaring at me from across the table, waiting for an answer.

"I don't want it to get stolen," I say.

"That's what a lock's for," says Annie.

"It's a rough school," I say. "I mean, it's okay and all, but there are kids who could chew a lock off a bicycle."

"A good source of iron," says Mum. Her voice sounds grouchy.

Annie keeps staring at me. I drink some orange juice. My hand shakes and she notices.

"You must get to school terribly early," says Mum. "You've been leaving here before eight."

I swallow. "Getting there early is a good way to meet people," I say. "Make friends."

"I have a friend," says Flora Bella. "Her name is Maisy. Her brother goes to Connaught; maybe you know him."

"What's his name?"

Flora Bella bites her tongue. "I don't know. But I'll ask and then you can become best friends just like Maisy and me."

"Maisy and I," says Mum.

"You don't even know her," says Flora Bella. She's got about an inch of lemon curd on her muffin and now she takes a big bite. Lemon curd drips onto her plate, her dress, the table. It looks like snot.

"I have a friend," says Annie.

Mum stops chopping and looks over at us.

"You do?" she says.

Annie is still staring at me like a python at a gerbil, so she doesn't notice the surprised look on Mum's face. "Her name is George," says Annie, "and she's really smart. Especially at science."

"That's wonderful, dear," says Mum. Then she glances at me with this little gleam of hope in her eyes.

"Maybe she could come over sometime," says Annie.

"Of course," says Mum.

"Good," says Annie. "And can we use the shed?"

"What for?"

"Science experiments."

"You're not going to make explosives, are you?"

"No," says Annie. "George's dad is a scientist at the experimental farm. We're doing botany experiments."

"Botany," says Mum as if it's the nicest word she's ever heard.

The whole time Annie's eyes have never left mine.

"I already asked if I could use the shed," I say.

"Well, too bad," says Annie.

"Mum?"

"Can't you share it?" says Mum. You'd think she'd know better.

"No," Annie and I say together. Then before I can say I asked first, Annie says, "You're so good at making *new* friends, Rex. When are you going to invite someone home?"

She's onto me. I don't know how, but she's onto me.

"Huh?"

"I didn't hear you."

"When I meet someone I like."

"Yeah, I guess you've already got so many friends, it's not a big deal making new ones."

"What's that supposed to mean?"

"Oh, nothing."

"Well then shut up!"

"Ow!" says Mum, and her paring knife clatters onto the cutting board. "Damnation!" she says, grabbing hold of her finger. She turns on the tap and holds her hand under it. Blood oozes from her finger.

"Are you okay, Mummy?" says Flora Bella.

"I thought so," she says. "I really thought so."

Annie's forehead wrinkles into a frown. I'm frowning, too. Mum's voice sounds wobbly all of a sudden, and it's my fault. I shouldn't have yelled at Annie, but I couldn't stop myself.

In my head, suddenly, there's this awful ruckus of beating wings and black feathers. More crows. The leafless tree is littered with them. How long will it take until a branch cracks?

◎ ◎ ◎

Sunday afternoon I look for Dad. He's reading *Time* magazine in his big old chair in a brand-new living room. I stand in front of him, waiting for him to notice me.

He doesn't for a long time, or at least he pretends not to. He's like that.

"Here's a brave lass," he says eventually. He holds up the magazine to show me a picture. There's a photograph of a Negro girl, a teenager, clutching her schoolbooks to her chest. There are policemen all around her and people holding signs. The girl has her head down.

"What did she do?"

"Went to school," says Dad. "A white school." He shakes his head. "Who would have ever thought getting an education could be so dangerous." Then he closes the magazine and looks at me. "What can I do for you, chum?"

"I need five dollars."

"Five dollars?"

"For a school project."

"Five dollars?"

"I'm going to make a piano."

"A five-dollar piano?"

"Out of balsa wood. I already costed it out." That gets his attention, just like I knew it would. Dad's an engineer and he costs out building projects. "I figured out how much lumber, glue, and paint I'd need and then I went to the hobby store to cost it out."

"Did you add ten percent to your calculations in case of mishaps?"

"Yes, sir."

"Good man. And it came to five dollars?"

"Four sixty-five. I'll bring you the change. Honest."

He nods. "Well, then," he says. "All right."

I breathe a sigh of relief. "Thanks."

"Your mother will be pleased. She's always wanted a piano."

"It's only going to be little, Dad."

"Yes, well she only wanted one a little."

Then he goes back to reading.

"Dad?"

He looks up. "What, you again?"

"The money?"

"Ah," he says. "Well, I can't give it to you now, Rex. It'll have to be next Friday."

"Next Friday?"

"I'm sorry, son. Your mother and I have budgeted down to the penny this month, what with back-to-school supplies and all the expenses of moving. I just don't have anything to spare. Not a sou, not a farthing, not a sparrow's fart."

I know it's not really an emergency, but I had wanted to start the piano right away.

"I get paid on Friday," he says. "Can you wait until then?"

◎ ◎ ◎

Monday, I decide to take my own money: five dollars' worth of pennies, nickels, dimes, and quarters. I'll still have enough left over to buy bus tickets to get me through the week and I don't want to wait until Friday. All the change weighs my pants down and makes a big fat bulge in my pocket.

I'm extra careful leaving for the bus Monday morning. I don't know for sure whether Annie's onto me, but I'm not taking any chances. So I head down Fairmont as if I were going to Connaught. Then, after checking behind me, I dash across Laurentian to Irving—clinking all the way—and up Irving to Carling Avenue where the bus stops.

When I finally get to school I see Stewart Lessieur and

take a good hard look at him. He's the one who thinks I'm an idiot—the guy who plays hockey with sixteen-year-olds and who I don't want as an enemy. He's over by the entrance of the school yard with two of his buddies. I don't know their names. The two buddies are pestering kids as they arrive at school, dancing around, blocking their way and threatening to steal stuff. One of the buddies is skinny with a blond pompadour like Bobby Rydell. He's wearing an electric yellow shirt and stick-thin black pants. He looks like a pencil. The other guy is small with a buzz cut, brown shirt, and tan pants. His arms jerk around like he's a monkey marionette and the puppeteer doesn't know what he's doing.

Stew squats by the fence watching his boys with a sneery smile on his face, like one of those dog owners who lets his mutt off its leash at the park and enjoys watching it knock kids off their trikes and steal their ice cream cones. Stew's black hair is done up in a ducktail and he's wearing this varsity jacket, black and gold. He's hunkered down like a catcher behind the plate, with his forearms resting on his knees, but with no glove.

"Stew," says Kathy. *"Spew."*

"So what do we call his two sidekicks?" says Buster.

"The skinny one is Puke," says Kathy. "The little monkey guy is Dribble."

A girl tries to get past Puke, her head down and clutching her books to her chest, and it reminds me of the Negro girl in *Time*. This girl is hurrying but trying not to run, as if she knows that running will only make things worse. She's trying to be brave as Puke pokes at her books and jumps in front of her, making faces.

"Why do people do that?" says James.

"Because they're bullies," says Kathy. She looks ready to go over and straighten Puke out.

"They're just looking for attention," says Polly.

"Well, I'll give him some attention," says Kathy. She rolls up the sleeves of her sweater, but Polly grabs her shoulder, won't let her go.

Polly has started hanging out with us sometimes, which is both great and terrifying. Now I want to roll up my sleeves like Gary Cooper and go and deal with those bullies across the yard myself, but I'm not even going to pretend to start to do it, because maybe Polly wouldn't stop me.

The crazy puppet guy steals this other boy's baseball cap and throws it to Spew.

"Creeps," says James.

Spew waggles the cap in front of the little kid, who darts around trying to grab it back but isn't fast enough.

"Why don't you pick on someone your own size," Kathy shouts, but we're too far away for him to hear. Which is just as well, I guess, but I hate it.

"He thinks he's so cool," says Buster.

"Aw, ignore them," says James. "They'll get tired of it sooner or later."

"He's a dork," says Kathy.

"Worse," says Polly. "He's an LMT."

"A what?"

"Lunch money thief," says Polly. "He'll get someone in a corner and they have to give him whatever they've got, or else. That's what I heard, anyway."

I slide my hand protectively down into my pocket. Why did I bring a pocketful of money to school today of all days?

It's Fate—that's what it is. It's a setup. The crows are laughing and hopping up and down on their branches. God is about to pay me back for all those lies.

I look up and then—right that very moment—Spew turns his gaze on me. Not us—me. It's almost as if he heard the money jingle as I wrapped my fingers around all those coins.

He stares right at me. He smiles, but it isn't a friendly smile. He says something out of the corner of his mouth and Puke looks at me and snorts.

I should look away but I can't. I don't know why. I just keep staring, as if I'm under some kind of a spell. Now Dribble joins the other two, laughing. Laughing at me. Then slowly, slowly Spew's eyes drift down my skinny chest until he's staring directly at my pocket: the one with the money in it. Way more than lunch money.

◎ ◎ ◎

I was going to go to Hobbyland after school. It's just a few blocks south of Hopewell, but there's no way now. Spew lives around here somewhere. That's what people say.

They've seen him in the school yard at night, playing ball hockey all alone. I'm not taking any chances. The way he looked at me, it was as if he had X-ray vision and could see clear through the bones of my hand. I'm a marked man.

I stick with my friends after school and we walk back over the canal into the Glebe, with me checking over my shoulder every few seconds.

"Relax," says Buster.

"That's easy for you to say," I mutter.

The closer we get to my old neighborhood, the safer I feel and the sadder I feel. I say goodbye to the guys at the corner of Clemow. I don't want to go up that street. Don't want to see 197. I drop into the Clemow Smoke Shop and exchange all my coins for a crisp five-dollar bill.

"My old friend, Zero," says Mr. Papazian. "How is it, your new home?"

We talk a bit. I don't tell him I'm going to Hopewell. He might start asking questions and I'm getting pretty tired of lying. I notice it's getting dark and I say goodbye, but as I'm about to leave I ask Mr. Papazian if there are any hobby shops nearby. He gets out the Yellow Pages, and sure enough, there's another place north on Bank Street, not far from where I have to catch the bus home.

"Zero," he says. "Come back here." Then he smiles and gives me a Bazooka Joe: something to chew on.

I buy my supplies at Handy Andy's, and just as I'm thinking things turned out all right, after all, there's a huge crack of thunder outside and the rain comes.

I should have known.

I pack what I can in my knapsack and carry the balsa wood in a long brown-paper sack that's drenched by the time I catch the number six. The bus is packed. It's rush hour already. I have to stand the whole way, squished between a woman with a very big bust and a guy carrying a huge parcel. It's still raining when I get off, but I don't even bother running. I'm too tired and wet. The sack holding the balsa wood has turned to brown-paper gunk by the time I reach the house.

I clamber up the steps and there on the porch swing waiting to greet me is Annie Oakley. She's not alone.

GEORGE

They're sitting on the wide porch swing.

"George, this is Rex. Rex, this is George." I'm kind of amazed. I didn't know Annie had ever learned any manners.

"Hi," I say.

"Hi," says George, waving a little wave. She's wearing a gray sweat suit I'm pretty sure is Annie's and Annie's fuzzy orange slippers. Annie is dressed in pajamas, a cardigan, and thick woolen socks.

"You look like a drowned cat," says Annie.

"We got caught in it, too, but not so bad," says George.

Annie's hair is one big fluff ball. George's hair is short but sort of spiky from being toweled dry, I guess. She wraps her arms around herself, her left hand rubbing her right arm. She looks kind of shy.

"We were working in the shed," says Annie. "Do not go in there!"

I don't have the energy for a fight.

"I think Rex just wants to go inside the house," says George gently. "He looks ready to drop."

"Okay," says Annie. And she makes a shooing gesture as if I'm some bothersome fly. That's more like the sister I know.

"Nice to meet you," I say to George.

She nods. Now her right hand is rubbing her left arm.

"She's staying for supper," says Annie.

"Well, see you later," I say, my hand on the doorknob.

"How's Hopewell treating you?" says Annie.

"It's okay," I say, without even thinking. And she's got me—just like that.

My hand falls from the doorknob. I turn to look at her. She's grinning with this evil gleam in her eyes.

My shoulders droop. I slouch the soaking knapsack off my back. "How'd you find out?"

"George used to go to Connaught."

"There's no one there named Mrs. Beauregard," says George, apologetically.

"At least not someone who has been there *forever*," says Annie, making inverted commas in the air around "forever." "I guessed you were going to Hopewell anyway," she says. "I knew you'd want to be with your precious little friends."

"Don't say that."

"Well, they are, aren't they? Anyway, George phoned the office at Hopewell."

"It was her idea," says George. "Sorry."

"She pretended she was the mother of a student who wanted to talk to Mrs. Beauregard. Her voice is more grownup sounding than mine."

"I wonder why," I mutter. But Annie is too pleased with herself to notice.

"When the secretary said she'd take a message, we just hung up. We knew all we needed to know."

I hang my head. Five days. That's all I managed.

"It's okay, Rex," says George. "Your secret is safe with us."

"Hey!" says Annie, punching her in the arm. "Don't say that." Then she turns to me. "I might tell, if I feel like it."

"Do whatever you want," I say.

"Just stay away from the shed. If I see you've been in there messing around, I'll tell Mum just like that." She clicks her fingers.

"That's pretty harsh," says George.

Annie grunts, as if she doesn't like it that George criticized her. Then she frowns at me as if it's my fault.

"So your friends must be in on this," she says. "Who'd have guessed they were so adventurous."

It almost sounds like a compliment, but she snatches it away pretty quick.

"One of them will snitch," she says.

"No they won't!" I say. "They're the best friends ever."

She smirks. "Whatever you say. But how, exactly, were you planning on handling parent-teacher interviews?"

I stand there, dumbstruck. Parent-teacher interviews?

"And what about getting your report card signed? Did you think of that?"

Now my shoulders really droop. I shake my head.

"Ah, lay off him," says George.

"It's all right," I say. "I'm used to her being mean." I glare at Annie and turn toward the door. But then I turn back to her. "It may have been stupid, okay. But I'm just so tired of moving."

"I know how you feel," says George. "My family moved a bunch of times."

"Her dad is a scientist at the Central Experimental Farm."

"I know," I snap. "You already told me."

"He studies plants," says Annie. Then she winks at her friend. "We're doing some botanical experiments ourselves, aren't we, Georgie?"

George looks uncomfortable. She has worried-looking eyes. Then she looks at me. "My family lived down in southern Ontario, and out west in Alberta, and in Ohio before that. It's tough."

Annie scowls. "The thing is," she says, "if you hadn't moved and we hadn't moved, you and I would never have met." Then she turns to me. "And if we hadn't moved from Vancouver, you'd have never met James and those other kids. Think about that."

I'd never thought about it before. She's right, in a way, but wrong in a whole bunch of ways I'm too tired to try to explain.

TWELVE

Annie doesn't rat on me. She acts like she's going to, just to watch me squirm. But after a while, I stop squirming and she stops pretending she's going to tell. She just looks at me like I'm a sap.

"You'll cave," she whispers.

"Will not."

"Will, too."

But I'm not going to cave. I got myself into this whole stupid mess and I'm staying in it. My parents never go to parent-teacher nights, anyway. And I'll forge Dad's signature on my report card if I have to. I've told so many lies now, who cares.

At school I play it cool, like Buster said I should. I do my work, but I don't try too hard or answer questions or offer to take a message to the office for Mrs. Beauregard. She looks a little disappointed, as if she made a mistake about me and I'm really just another lump. She calls most of the boys lumps, and most of the girls bumps. I don't know why and I don't care. This is my school and no one is going to change that. So I keep my head down, especially when Spew Lessieur is around. Every now and then I catch him looking at me with this look on his face as if he's got plans for me. Well, I'm ready. Sort of.

One thing for sure is I don't carry any money on me, which is easy really, because I hardly have any. I phone the *Ottawa Citizen* and the *Ottawa Journal* about getting a paper route, but I learn that I'd have to get up in the middle of the night to do my route and still get to school on time. James says they have jobs for pin boys down at the bowling alley. That would be great—sitting in the little room behind the pins, standing them back up and dodging bowling balls! But when I check into it, the hours are no good there, either. Saturday would be okay but I'll have to wait in line for a Saturday slot to open up. I leave my name with the boss, but he doesn't sound too hopeful.

Two good things happen. I start making the piano. I bought this great little saw at the hobby shop that's especially made for balsa wood and it cuts really, really clean. I also bought two grades of sandpaper: fine and finer. This is going to be the best thing I ever made.

The other good thing is that the gang was planning to go to a movie Saturday and Kathy asked Polly if she'd come. Polly said yes! James and I want to see *Jason and the Argo-*

nauts at the Mayfair; Buster, Kathy, and Polly want to see *The Nutty Professor* at the Somerset. They win. I don't care. We could see a documentary on clothespins and it would be fine.

◎ ◎ ◎

Friday comes at last, with no more calamities. Annie is hardly around anymore, because of George, so it's like a vacation around our place. There's a sign on the shed door that says: "KEEP OUT—THIS MEANS YOU REX!" She's probably booby-trapped the place.

When I get home from school, I go straight to my room and work on my piano. At five-thirty, I charge downstairs to greet Dad when he gets home from work. I sit out on the front porch, waiting for him. It's getting to feel like fall, but the light is pretty sifting through the trees. A few leaves are turning.

I sit with my feet a foot apart, my arms out straight as if I'm water-skiing. I look over and Polly is water-skiing beside me, like in those movies. We wave at each other and then do a complicated crossover pattern bouncing over each other's wake. The crowd loves us!

Six o'clock rolls around and Dad isn't home yet. Maybe he's always late on payday because of going to the bank or something. I hope he hasn't forgotten about the five dollars. I've got seventy-eight cents left in my piggy bank. And there's the movie tomorrow, which I hadn't counted on. I go in to find Mum. The calamity that hasn't happened all week is waiting for me.

"He's what?"

"He's on his way down to Belleville."

"Where's that?"

"Near Belle Town and Belle Crossing and Belle Junction. I don't know, Rex. All I know is that a bridge collapsed. No one was hurt, thank the Lord, but it's quite a schmozzle."

My head reels. I'm just about to start whining when I catch myself. Mum is not going to pay any attention to a whiner right about now, so I'd better think this through.

"Do you need any help with supper?" I ask.

She does. So far so good. I set the table, which is really Annie's job, except she's at George's for a sleepover. I help cut up vegetables, and when the Sausage comes in moaning about being hungry, I play Dinky Toys with him at the kitchen table. Mum looks over and smiles, which she doesn't do much these days. I thought she was upset about moving, but here we are, pretty well all moved in, and she's still tired and weird. Anyway, she seems okay right now.

"Did Dad say anything about five dollars?" I say nonchalantly.

She looks at me quizzically. "Not that I recall. Then again, with a million-dollar bridge collapsing, it probably wasn't high on his order of priorities."

The Sausage is running a tiny green Austin Healey up

my arm, chased by a tiny red Rover. "You're my mountain, Rex," he says. I want to swat the cars—pretend I'm an avalanche—but that might ruin things.

"But Dad's going to be back, right?"

"Eventually," she says. She's pouring water from a pot of potatoes into the sink and her face is lost in steam. "He said something about wanting to be home before you've all graduated from college."

"Mum."

She puts down the pot and turns to me, wiping her hands on her apron.

"Rex, I have no idea what you're getting at, so you'd better speak plainly."

It's hard to speak plainly when your little brother is having a car race over your body, but I try my best. I tell Mum about the project money and how Dad was going to give me five dollars today. I really work at keeping my voice calm. Meanwhile, Mum turns back to the counter to smush potatoes and mix gravy and I'm not even sure she's listening.

"So what do you think?" I say after a while.

She counts the bowls of food on the counter in case she's forgotten anything.

"Mum?"

She finally turns back to me and the look on her face makes me wish she'd go back to smushing potatoes.

"What is this obsession with money?" she says.

"It's not an obsession."

"Yes, it is. You're always rooting about and pestering. I've never known you to be so money-conscious. Five dollars?"

"It's for a—"

She gasps, covers her mouth with her hand. "It's this new school, isn't it."

"What?"

"There's some awful gang of delinquents demanding money from you."

"No, there isn't."

"I saw something like this on television. Is it extortion, Rex? You must tell me."

"What's extor—"

"Oh, Lord," she says, wandering over and sitting down across the kitchen table from me, as if she's suddenly too weak to stand. "The school could be a den of thieves for all I know. I haven't even seen the place."

"Mum, it's not like that—"

"What kind of a mother am I?" she says. She's wringing her dishcloth.

"Mum, the money is for a school project. That's all."

But it's no use. She's not listening. The Sausage starts racing a Dinky Toy up her arm and she doesn't even notice.

"How am I going to do this?" she says.

"Do what?"

"All this and . . . oh, never mind."

She looks at me and then at the Sausage. She pulls him onto her lap and gives him a big hug.

"You're squashing my car," says the Sausage. But she's off somewhere else by now. Just gone.

◎ ◎ ◎

I pour the money out of my piggy bank onto the bed. Still only seventy-eight cents. The movie would cost a quarter. I could go without popcorn or candy, but if Polly is coming, I'd better have an extra quarter just in case. I mean, maybe she'll want some licorice? So I'd better take another quarter. Which is okay, because even then I'll have enough money to get bus tickets for Monday and Tuesday.

I hope they can get that bridge fixed by then.

◎ ◎ ◎

In the end, Buster can't make it, so it's James and Kathy, and Polly and me. Sort of like a double date. Gulp! Polly wears a green tartan dress with a green velvet belt and a velvet collar, and green velvet ribbons in her hair. We share a box of Maltesers, her favorite. At one point we both rest our arms on the armrests at the same time and they are less than one one-millionth of an inch apart. All the hairs on my arm stand up.

I walk her home. We all walk together, but it ends up me and her and James and Kathy, just like a real date. I can't think of anything to say. We could talk about the movie, I guess, but I don't remember anything about it.

"Have you thought of what you're going to do for the music project?" she says finally.

I look at her in disbelief. "Have you?"

She nods. "I know it's kind of early," she says.

"No!" I say. "Not if you want to do something really good."

She looks at me with her beautiful green eyes as if doing something really good was just what she had in mind.

She swallows. "I've decided to learn something really hard on the flute. It's a *Fantasie* by Gabriel Fauré. In E minor." Then she laughs nervously.

"E minor must be hard."

"I knew you'd understand," she says, "being a singer, and all."

A singer and all.

"Actually, I'm only learning one small part of it. But some of the fingering is a little bit tricky," she says. "That's why I started learning it early." She smiles at me. "What are you going to do?" she asks.

"I'm making a piano," I say proudly.

"A piano? You're making a piano?"

"Yes," I say. "It's a miniature one. I measured the piano in the music room and I'm making an exact replica."

She looks impressed. Awestruck. I want to tell her that it's almost finished, but I stop myself. I don't want to jinx it.

We walk in silence for a bit. Then she says, "My name's not really Polly."

"It isn't?"

She shakes her head. "It's Pearl. After my grandmother."

"Wow! Pearl is a beautiful name. Except for Pearl Harbor."

I wish I hadn't said that, but she just swallows again. Then she holds her hand to her throat and makes a little throat-clearing noise, but in a nice way. Unless maybe she's got a Malteser stuck down there.

"My last name isn't really Norton-Norton," I say after a while, just in case she's still thinking of what I said about Pearl Harbor.

Now a smile lights up her face. I've heard that expression before but I've never seen it really happen.

"I know," she says. "Everyone calls you Rex Zero."

The next thing I know, she's counting on her fingers.

"What are you doing?" I ask.

"I'm figuring out what the numerological value of Rex Zero is."

"Oh." I don't know what she's talking about, but I don't want to ask, in case it's something I should know already.

"It's twelve," she says finally. "R-E-X is 9-5-6. And Z-E-R-O is 8-5-9-6. Which adds up to twenty and twenty-eight, which makes forty-eight. Then you add four plus eight and get twelve. I think." She laughs nervously again. "Math isn't my best subject."

"It sounded okay to me," I say. "Is twelve good?"

She shrugs. "I only know up to ten but I'll try to find out."

"I hope twelve is good," I say. But she doesn't answer. Her face has gone bright red now, and I'm a little worried. I hope it isn't a Malteser stuck in her throat. Luckily, Kathy is with us and her mother is a nurse.

I turn around to look, just in case, and Kathy and James are gone. When did that happen?

It isn't a Malteser. When I ask her, she laughs and says I'm funny. Then we're at her house and she says, "See you Monday."

And I say, "You bet."

I have to go get my bike at James's house. Then I head home, thinking of Polly and me playing a duet: her on flute and me on my tiny piano.

There's no way I'm leaving Hopewell now. Not ever!

THE FIRST CRACK

James and I go to Buster's place Tuesday after school, to check out his new portable record player. He bought three 45s: "Blue Velvet," "My Boyfriend's Back," and "If I Had a Hammer"—numbers one, two, and three on the Platter Poll in the *Ottawa Citizen*. We're having a good time, but I'm so anxious about Dad getting back that I head home early.

No Dad. He won't be home until tomorrow. I officially have no money to buy tickets for the bus.

I check everywhere: every counter, under every cushion, out on the street. I check the front door stoop in case the milkman left change one morning and some of it rolled away. Technically, that wouldn't be stealing, would it?

What am I going to do? I could bike to school, I guess, but it would take almost an hour and the weather has turned awful. The wind is up: probably a thunderstorm brewing. A hurricane.

The wrath of God.

Tuesday night I put a third coat of black enamel paint on my piano. It shines like a concert grand, even though it's only an upright. And it's only eight inches tall.

I painted the keys white—well, the white keys, anyway. I couldn't fit eighty-eight, but I got a fair number. I used my skinniest paintbrush from an old paint-by-numbers kit. For a little while I thought about making every key a different color—a rainbow piano! But then I thought of Miss Hotchkiss and I knew she would want my piano to be as real-looking as possible.

But how am I going to get it to school if I have no money? It's not due for weeks, but now that it's done, I can't wait to show it to Polly. It's all I can think about.

You made this, Rex? By yourself? I can't believe it. You are the most talented person I have ever met.

I lie down on my bed, my hands behind my head. I try to tell myself I could just stay home tomorrow. I could pretend I was sick and wait until Dad gets back with my five dollars. No. I've already got way too many things to pretend, and anyway, I've never felt so unsick in my life. How can I keep away from school when Polly is there?

I think about phoning her to tell her I'm bringing my piano. I've never phoned her before, but this would be a good excuse. I run downstairs and find Letitia on the phone. I try to get her to hurry up but she just turns away and turns away again until she's completely wrapped herself up in the telephone cord. It's already almost nine o'clock.

She smiles and nods at me, but doesn't hurry one bit. Even when I get down on the floor and plead.

Finally, at 9:06 p.m., she finishes her call.

"It's all yours, Rexarino," she says, unwrapping herself from the cord.

I look up Polly's number. I pick up the phone. Then I freeze. Will she think I'm showing off bringing in my project so early? Maybe she'll be disappointed to find out it's only a pretend piano? I hang up the phone and stare at it. Maybe she's not allowed to talk on the phone at night? Some kids aren't. Maybe she's one of those kids with really strict parents and I'll end up getting her in trouble? I don't want to do that.

"What are you doing?" It's Annie.

"None of your business," I say.

"Phoning one of your little friends?" she says. Then she leans in close to my ear and whispers, "At Hopewell Avenue School."

I jump up to get away, flapping my hand by my ear in case any cooties jumped off her.

The second I get up, she slips into my place and picks up the phone.

"Thanks," she says.

She is so horrible I could scream.

I don't phone Polly. It'll be better if it's a surprise. So I'm lying on my bed trying to think of how I'll get to school the next day, when a vision comes into my head of the little telephone table down in the front hall. Next to it is a ladder-backed chair. And hanging over the back of the chair is my mother's handbag.

I look at the clock on my bedside table. It's nine-thirty. Mum, Letitia, and Annie will be up for hours. I was right there only a few minutes ago. I could have done it. I mean, I only need a quarter.

I close my eyes. *Just one quarter.* And it would only be a loan. I could pay Mum back once Dad gives me the money he owes me. That's what I tell myself. But I've never stolen money in my life.

It's not just the stealing. It's Mum's purse. We are not allowed to go into Mum's purse for anything, ever. We have to take the purse to her and let her find it. I remember once thinking maybe she had a gun in there and she didn't want us to find it. But even that wasn't a good enough reason to take a look.

I open my eyes, look at my clock. I pick it up and set the alarm to ring at six-thirty a.m. What else can I do?

When I close my eyes, another crow lands softly on the largest branch of the tree in my head. The dead and leafless tree of lies. The other crows hop along to make room for him. There are a hundred crows on that branch—maybe two hundred. And as he lands, I hear it—the first crack.

THE VISE

The scariest intro to any show on TV is for *The Vise*. There's this silhouette of a guy standing in the jaws of a huge vise. The screw is turning, the vise is closing, and the guy is waving his arms in the air because he can't move and soon . . . soon . . .

I wake up in a sweat all tied up in my bedclothes. I look at the clock: 6:29. I push down the plunger so the alarm doesn't ring. How does the body know how to do that—wake up at exactly the right time?

I lie there and feel my eyes slowly close again. "How will you get your piano to school?" a little voice in my head says. "On the bus," I answer. "How?" "I'll borrow some money from my mother's purse." "That's not what I mean. How?" says the voice in my head. He thinks I'm an idiot, too. "I'll take it in my knapsack, of course," I answer. "Oh, really?" says the little voice. Which is when my eyes snap open.

I left my knapsack at Buster's!

I look across the room and there's my piano just visible in the dim light. I scoot out of bed, tiptoe across the room, and pick it up. The house is dead quiet. The floor is cold on my bare feet. I put the piano down carefully on my desk. I find my slippers, tiptoe to the bedroom door, and peer out onto the landing. There's just Annie's room and mine on the third floor. Her door is closed. All is quiet below. I move like a thief down the staircase to the second floor. I stop and listen. Still no movement, except for the sounds a grumpy old house makes in its sleep.

I tiptoe down to the first floor. There I am, alone, in the wide front hall, and there is my target: Mum's purse, as shiny and black as my piano.

I can't move. It's like my feet are stuck in concrete. I can feel the vise tightening. I see that tiny little silhouette of a man waving his arms in the air—and his face is mine!

I take a deep breath. It's now or never. I look up the stairs one last time, then dive my hand, slowly, way down into the bag. I pretend my hand is Lloyd Bridges in *Sea Hunt*, swimming deeper and deeper into the sea. Past the barnacle-covered wallet, past schools of brightly colored discount vouchers and long wavy fronds of handkerchief. Finally, I'm at the bottom where treasure lies amid the peppermint crabs and hairpin clams. A quarter.

"What are you doing?"

I freeze. Then slowly, slowly slip my hand out of the bag clutching the quarter tightly. Not too fast, or I might get the bends!

I turn. It's Annie Oakley. She's standing on the last stair.

"I'm telling," she says.

"You said you wouldn't."

"I'm not going to tell on you for going to Hopewell. I'm going to tell on you for stealing."

"Shhhh. I am not. Mum forgot to give me my allowance."

"Liar." She glares at me. "Anyway, you know the rules about Mum's purse."

"It's urgent," I whisper. I show her the quarter. "It's just a loan. Dad owes me some money."

"Liar."

"It's true!"

"How about I just go wake up Mum, right now?"

Annie turns as if to go back up the stairs. But she pauses. She wants me to fall on my knees and beg—promise I'll do the dishes for six years if she doesn't tell.

But I don't fall for it. She looks over her shoulder at me and I meet her gaze like a gunfighter. And that's when I notice her getup. She's in ratty old pedal pushers and scuffed-up running shoes. She's got a brown-paper shopping bag under her arm full of something.

"Where are *you* going?" I ask her.

"Don't change the subject."

"What are you doing in pants on a school day?"

"I've got my school clothes in here," she says, squeezing the bag tighter.

"You're skipping school," I say.

"I am not! I'm going to George's," she whispers. "There are some plants we have to pick."

"Now who's the liar?"

"It's true."

"I don't believe you."

She stamps her foot silently on the carpeted stair. Then, before I know what's happening, she jumps down the last step, crosses the floor, and takes me by the scruff of my pajamas.

"You're the one who's lying," she says. "And I'm telling."

"Be my guest," I say, more bravely than I feel. "Or are you in too big a hurry?"

She shakes me a bit, like a dog shaking a bone, and then we both hear a door open, footsteps, the bathroom door opening and closing. Mum.

Annie lets go of me and heads for the front door.

"Tonight!" she whispers, stabbing a finger in my direction.

"If you tell on me, I'll tell on you," I say, racing after her. She smiles her most evil smile.

"You don't have a leg to stand on, Rex *Zero*," she says. Then she shuts the door silently.

I watch her through the window skipping down the steps to the street.

Upstairs, the toilet flushes and the whole house kind of judders like the *Titanic* just hit an iceberg. Mum heads back to her room. I don't want to be standing around the hall with stolen money in my hand when she comes down.

At least Annie's brown-paper bag gives me an idea. There's a drawer in the kitchen filled with paper bags and I find one just the right size for a piano. I take a roll of toilet paper from the downstairs bathroom for padding. Then I scoot upstairs to get ready.

When I finally come down for breakfast, Mum's not there. There's just Letitia sitting at the table cutting up toast soldiers for the Sausage, who is still in his red all-in-ones, talking to his soft-boiled egg. The egg seems to be named Richard. Letitia is singing "Goodnight my someone, goodnight my love." It's kind of a weird song to sing first thing in the morning. Then again, it might not be morning on whatever planet Letitia lives on.

The only other person in the kitchen is Flora Bella, who is standing on the counter by the sink. She's looking through Dad's old army field glasses out the window.

"What are you doing?"

"Watching Mum."

"Mum's in the garden?"

"Uh-huh. She's on fire."

I rush over to the sink. "She's what?"

"There's smoke coming out the top of her head."

There's a chair where Flora Bella climbed onto the counter, and now I climb up after her, teeter a bit, and then snatch the field glasses away from her.

"Holy moly!"

"See? What did I tell you?"

"She's not on fire. She's smoking."

Letitia stops singing. "Mum is smoking?"

Flora Bella tries to grab the binoculars back from me and almost falls off the counter. I catch her by the arm but she ends up stepping into the sink, which is full of dirty dishwater. She sits down on the counter and sulks. And I go back to looking at our mother who never used to smoke.

She's standing at the end of the garden by the shed. She's looking out over the wall at the alley. She's not even dressed. She's in her floral housecoat and a pair of black Wellingtons. She puts out the cigarette, then leans on the wall, her head resting on her folded arms. Even though I can't see her face, I can tell she's unhappy.

"Is Mummy coming back?" asks the Sausage. He's got a toast soldier in each hand and his face is smeared with egg yolk. He looks like he's going to cry, but then he usually does.

"Of course she is," I say. "Don't be stupid."

I look out the window again. There's only one conclusion I can come to. She's found out about me. I've driven her to smoke.

DISASTER STRIKES

I don't want to be there when Mum comes back in the house. I eat a piece of bread and marmalade, but the butter is hard and gouges a hole in the bread. The marmalade falls through it onto my shirt and I give up after only two bites. I look in the fridge hoping there might be a lunch already made, like usual, the top of the bag neatly folded with a red R crayoned on the front. Nothing. So I grab an apple and head off. But I can't put my apple in the bag with the piano and it won't fit in my pocket, so I leave it on the telephone table in the hall. Mum's black purse hangs there, throbbing like it contains a horror-show heart.

I race up the street and wait for the number six. I check my watch. The bus is late. Finally it comes. I climb aboard and give the man my quarter. He looks at it funny and then gives it a sniff. "Did you steal this from your mother's purse?" he asks.

That's not what really happens. He just gives me four tickets and I shove one in the box and ask for a transfer.

The driver laughs. "You mean a transfer to *Hell*?"

I sit and look out the window. It's cloudy.

Annie will tell. She'll wait until dinner when everyone's together. And everyone will gasp. Dad, if he's back, will look pained the way he does when the old shrapnel wound in his knee is aching. Mum will pull out a pack of cigarettes and start smoking right there at the table. The Sausage will probably start choking, but Mum won't pat his back and he'll just die. Letitia will look at me with such sorrowful eyes. "Oh, Rex," she'll say sadly. Then she'll sing some song about people who steal things and go to Hell. Flora Bella will probably jump up and go and steal some money from Mum's purse, too. She always copies me. And then Mum will put her cigarette out in her mashed potatoes and say, "Now look what you've done, Rex."

"Bank Street."

I jump up, pull the cord, and make my way off the bus, but I'm too late to catch the number two. It's already leaving the corner, heading south. The passengers stare out their windows at me.

When I finally get to Hopewell, there's only ten minutes until the bell. I find James, Buster, and Kathy. They look pretty excited about something. But all I can think of is that Polly is missing.

"Kathy's mother is pregnant," says James.

"Yeah," says Buster. "With a baby."

"Really?"

Kathy nods. She looks pleased. A year ago she was angry that her mother was even dating someone. Things sure can change.

"That's great," I say.

Kathy frowns at me. "Are you okay?"

"Oh, sure," I say. "Uh, where's Polly?"

"Didn't she phone you?" Kathy asks.

"No."

"She was going to. Anyway, she's away for Jewish New Year. It's not until tomorrow, but they're going down to Cleveland."

"Cleveland?"

"Or somewhere. She didn't phone you?"

I shake my head. She probably did, but people were on the phone all night at my place. Why didn't I phone her? *What is wrong with me?*

"You look mad," says Kathy. "Aren't you happy for me?"

For a moment, I don't know what she means.

"The baby?"

"Oh, yeah," I say. "Of course. That's great. Really great."

"What's it going to be?" asks Buster. "The baby, I mean."

James says, "Oh, it'll probably be a boy if it isn't a girl."

"No, what I meant was, what do you hope it will be?"

Kathy thinks. "Well, I've already got a little stepsister, and she's okay. So I guess what I want is a brother." Then she beams at us: at me, at Buster, and last of all at James. He blushes and looks away.

"Hey," he says. "That's a big lunch, Rex."

I hold up my bag of piano. The paper bag is kind of bulgy from all the toilet paper stuffing.

"Whoa!" says Buster.

"It's actually a piano," I say. I unfold the top and clear away the toilet paper to show them.

"Miss KissKiss is going to give you an A-plus-plus," says James.

"She'll probably marry you," says Buster.

"It looks so real," says Kathy. She reaches into the bag and strokes the gleaming black top.

"Play something," says Buster. Then he suddenly glances behind me and his eyes get big. Before I can turn, someone pokes me hard in the shoulder.

I lurch—almost drop my bag. Then I turn around. It's him. Spew Lessieur.

"What's for lunch, small stuff?" he says.

"None of your business," says Kathy, punching him in the arm.

"Owww!" He rubs his arm as if it really hurts. Puke and Dribble laugh. But Spew isn't laughing. He looks at me hard, all the pimples around his mouth flaring up. Up close his gold and black varsity jacket looks old and way too big for him, even though he's so big himself. The leather is cracked, the wool of the arms is frayed in places.

"I asked you a question," he says, poking me again.

"It's a piano," I tell him, folding the top closed, extra tight.

"Did I ask for a funny man?" he says.

"Yeah," says Dribble. "Did he ask for a funny man?"

"I'm not being funny," I say. "It really is a piano."

"You think you're a funny man?" says Puke.

Even though I'm frightened, I have to roll my eyes.

"It's a model piano," says James. "A project for music class."

"Who asked you, Egghead?" says Spew. Then he looks at me. "Let me see," he says. I cradle the bag closer. "I just want to take a look," he says, his voice getting crabby.

I step backward, wrapping myself around the bag.

"You are making a big mistake," says Puke.

What's new, I think.

"Don't be such a snob," says Spew.

"I'm not a snob."

"I'm not a snob," echoes Puke, making a stupid face.

"You think you're something special?" Spew asks. "Always so nice in class, with your fancy-ass accent and big words?"

I'm stunned. And that's when Spew makes his move. He takes a swipe at my bag. I see it coming and step aside.

"Why don't you go back to your cage," says Buster, stepping between Spew and me, but Spew just shoves him out of the way, and now he's really mad. He's just about to grab the bag from me, when Kathy boots him in the back-side, hard.

He grabs hold of his bum with both hands.

I can't help it. I start laughing. Not just laughing, either. Crazy laughing. I'm exploding like a volcano. Maybe it's lack of sleep. Maybe I'm going crazy.

Everyone stares at me. Even Spew looks surprised. Then—lightning quick—he yanks the bag out of my hands.

Buster tries to get it back, but Puke nabs him and drags him off. Then Dribble jumps in front of Kathy and James, waving his crazy monkey arms in their faces. So it's just me and Spew and he's got my piano and suddenly it's as if the crazy laughter was just the smoke from that volcano inside me and now the lava comes pouring out.

"Give it back!" I shout, and grab for the bag.

"Why should I?" he says, holding the bag up too high for me.

The volcano blows. Maybe it's all the lies bubbling up in my gut. Maybe it's Polly not being here. Maybe it's the unfairness of the whole world, but—*Boom!*—I'm ballistic.

"Give. It. Back. *Now*, Spew!

"What'd you call me?"

"I called you *Spew*, like barf, like sick, because that's what you are." Then I lower my head and charge him. It happens so fast he can't get out of my way, and the next thing I know I'm driving him backward, my head buried in his stomach. I'm a battering ram.

Bang!

He's up against the chain-link fence and I can feel this huge oomph of air come out of him. I can smell it, too. I have to grab hold of my head with both hands because it hurts so much from clanging against his ribs. I step back, kind of dizzy, and watch Spew slide slowly down the fence, all the way to the ground.

Which is when I hear the crunch.

"What's going on over here?"

It's the school yard monitor and he's got his hand on me, but I tear myself free, push Spew out of the way, and kneel on the asphalt. I pick up the squashed bag he landed on.

I don't need to look inside. I can feel what's in there. Bones. Piano bones.

I hit Spew with the bag, battering him over the head, again and again, hitting him with my beautiful broken piano, screaming at him, until someone—I don't even know who—drags me off.

I'm sitting in homeroom just after the national anthem, when the call comes from the principal's office.

THE SECRET STUDENT

've never seen Mr. Tibbitts up close. He's not really scary, for a principal. His glasses are a little bit scary, but he's not. It looks as if he cut his chin shaving this morning, and there's a glassy yellow spot on his gray tie that looks like egg yolk.

"Rex," he says, after he finishes shuffling some papers on his desk. "Do you live at 197 Clemow Avenue?"

This is not what I expected.

"Well?"

I nod, just once. I don't seem to be able to speak.

"Was that a yes?"

I look down at my shoes. One of my laces is undone and I think about tying it.

"Rex?"

"Uh, yes. Yes it was a yes, sir. Yes."

Mr. Tibbitts frowns. "Well, that's mighty strange," he says, scratching his chin, "because Mrs. Swallow out there in the front office noticed today that the Madden girls also live at 197 Clemow Avenue. They've just moved back to Canada from overseas. Now, I happen to know the Madden girls have a younger brother, which means there are five of them in the family. How many people are there in your family, Rex?"

If I bend down to tie my shoelace, I'll be below the surface of Mr. Tibbitts's big brown desk. Maybe I could just crawl out of the office without him noticing.

"Rex?"

"Eight, sir. Well, actually only seven since my sister got married last June."

"Hmmm," says Mr. Tibbitts. "That house on Clemow must be a whopper."

"Yes, sir."

"And speaking of whoppers," he says. But he doesn't go on. He tilts his head up and the light catches his glasses and makes me blink.

He doesn't look very happy.

"The thing is, Rex, when we phoned your number to check up on this, the operator came on and gave us a new listing, a Pacific listing: PA 7-8001. That's in the west end, isn't it?"

I can't look at him.

"Rex, could you please pay attention?"

"Sorry, sir."

"I want to know what's going on."

He sounds harsher now, as if he's used up his daily supply of kindness.

I take a deep breath. By dinner I'll be a dead man, since Annie was going to tell on me anyway. How much deader can you be than dead?

"We moved, sir. But it was after my other school already sent you those thingies—"

"Transcripts?"

"Transcripts, right, and so I figured it would be okay to come here to Hopewell because it was where all my friends were going and . . ."

He waits for more but there isn't any.

"So your father drives you in every morning?"

"Not exactly."

"Your mother?"

"No, sir. But it's not hard to get here. Two buses, the number six and—"

"Do your parents know about this, Rex?"

I take another deep breath, but there doesn't seem to be enough air in the principal's office to go around.

"No, sir." My voice sounds like a gerbil's.

Mr. Tibbitts clears his throat. I look up. His hands are linked together and it's surprising how much hair he has on his knuckles considering how little he has on his head.

"I tried to call your house this morning, but nobody seems to be home."

I'm not really surprised. They probably moved again.

"You do realize that you can't stay here, Rex, don't you?"

There's a little notch on the front end of his desktop like maybe a kid sitting in this chair had a penknife and carved it for something to do while the principal was yelling at him. I want to reach out and feel it, but I hold back.

"Rex, I'm talking to you. This is a serious matter."

"Yes, Mr. Tibbitts, sir. I'm sorry. I just feel a little . . ."

"A little what?"

I shrug. "We move so much. I've lived in more houses than I've had grades of school." I look up at him and he leans forward a bit, so the glare goes from his glasses and I can see his eyes, soft gray eyes, the same shade as his tie. "I didn't mean to trick anyone. Things just got out of hand. And, anyway, nobody said I *couldn't* go to Hopewell and I really like it here and my friends—well, they're the best friends I ever had."

There. I've said it. It's all I can say.

He burps, quietly, raising his fist to cover his mouth. He looks down at the papers on his desk, his hands open like a magician who has just made something disappear before your eyes.

"Well, Rex, I'm sorry about that. Life can be pretty hard. But there's a reason we have school districts."

"What is it, sir?"

"Excuse me?"

"Why *do* we have school districts?"

"Well, things would be chaotic, Rex, if we didn't have boundaries and districts. People start choosing where they want to go—where they feel like going for who knows what reasons, and—"

"I'm a pretty good student," I say, interrupting him. Hey, what have I got to lose? "Apart from what happened this morning, which wasn't really my fault, because Spew—I mean Stewart Lessieur—destroyed my piano."

"What are you talking about?"

"Nothing, sir. I just mean I'm not taking someone else's place here, am I? Why couldn't I stay?"

The phone rings and Mrs. Swallow's voice comes over the intercom. "It's Partridge for you, sir."

"Ah," he says. "Just the man I was waiting for."

Mr. Tibbitts picks up the phone and I sit back in my chair, my hands squeezed tightly together between my thighs. He's cross with me, I know, but he seems like a nice enough person. Maybe if I talk to him politely. Maybe if he talks to my teachers and finds out how good a student I am.

But when Mr. Tibbitts puts the phone back on the receiver, he's all business.

"I'm not sure if you were listening to that call, Rex, but it was Mr. Partridge at Connaught School out in your neck of the woods. He's a good man, runs a tight ship."

"Sir?"

"Connaught is where you should be, Rex. And that's where you will be, as of Monday next. Fine school. We'll be sending over your transcripts this afternoon. Meanwhile,

I'll keep trying to reach your parents. Does your mother work?"

"Well, we have a big house—"

"I mean is she gainfully employed?"

Gainfully?

"Rex. Have you any idea when your mother will be home?"

I shake my head. She's probably at the end of the garden, smoking.

"No idea at all, sir." And then without him saying that I'm excused, I just get up and leave.

What's he going to do—give me detention?

HOME

When I get home, no one's there, but I recognize the furniture, so that's something, I guess. I head to the kitchen and have a big bowl of Froot Loops with chocolate milk. Then I have another, and a glass of orange juice and a banana and a piece of apple pie left over from dinner. I'm still hungry. It's as if there's this big black hole inside me. Then I feel sleepy from all that food, so I drag myself up two flights of stairs and keel over on my bed.

I wake up to the sound of crying. It's the Sausage. I listen and it sounds like Mum is putting him down for a nap. My clock says it's a few minutes past noon. I know I should probably tell Mum I'm home but I don't. I just lie there with my head on my arm staring at my desk—staring at the place where my perfect little piano stood just a few hours ago, all black and shining.

Beating up the biggest bully in the school yard probably wasn't such a good idea, now that I think about it, but

I'm never going to see him again anyway. It's not my school yard anymore.

Next thing I know, I'm waking up again, this time to the distant sound of the telephone.

I wait and wait. Fifteen minutes pass. Finally I hear Mum's footsteps on the stairway up to my room. She's walking slowly, like maybe she's dragging some huge club after her like Alley Oop in the funny pages.

She knocks on my door.

"Rex? Are you there?"

I don't say anything.

"Rex?"

"I'm not here," I say. "I'm at school."

She waits a moment longer, then opens the door and comes in.

"I've just been talking to Mr. Tibbitts," she says.

"Who's that?" I ask.

"Your principal."

"Oh. I thought Mr. Tibbitts was the principal at Hope-well Avenue School in Ottawa South. My principal's name is . . . I don't remember, but he runs a tight ship."

Mum doesn't say anything for a minute. She's got a tissue in her hand, all wadded up, and I look at her face to see if she's been crying. Her eyes do look a bit red. "I'm sorry," I mutter, but all I really feel is sorry for myself.

She finally sits on the edge of the bed. "I'm the one who should be saying I'm sorry," she says. "I don't know how we could have ever let this happen."

I stare at her. How come adults are so hard to figure out? She's apologizing to *me*? I stare until Mum looks away.

"Things have been so . . . so hard, lately," she says. "What with the wedding and moving yet again and . . . well, I've kind of let things go."

Now I *really* should be saying something. If I were Beaver Cleaver, I'd sit up right away and say, "It's okay, Mom. It's me who was being bad." And then Mrs. Cleaver would probably say "*I*, Beaver." And I'd say "No, *me*." And she'd laugh and say, "I'm talking about bad grammar, not bad behavior." And then Beav would say "Oh," the way he does, and the studio audience would have a good little laugh. Except there is no studio audience in my room, just silence, and the silence is really getting loud.

I sink back into my pillow. "I might as well tell you this now because Annie is going to tell you anyway. I took a quarter from your purse to buy bus tickets this morning." I peek through my fingers.

"Is this the first time?"

I nod. "I saved up money like crazy all summer but it ran out when I had to buy the stuff for this school project."

"Which is why you needed the five dollars?"

"Yes, ma'am."

She sighs again and wearily shakes her head.

"I'm sorry I've been bad. I know it's probably because of me that you started smoking."

"I beg your pardon?" Every muscle on her face looks as

if it's ready to go *sproing* like a bunch of stretched rubber bands.

"I just thought—"

"You just thought," she says. *Sproing!* "I wish I could do anything—*anything at all*—without everyone knowing about it." *Sproing!*

Wow! I don't even know what we're talking about anymore, but I figure I'd better shut up.

"I have *no* secrets," she says. "I don't have secrets—all I have is children. An endless number of children." Then her voice breaks and she sort of caves in.

Time passes. The Egyptians build another pyramid or two. Russia launches another Sputnik. Then she shudders and the spell has passed. She sniffs.

"We'll get you sorted out at Connaught on Monday. I had a good talk with Mr. Tibbitts, *and* with Mr. Partridge, as well."

That's his name: my new principal, the one with the tight ship. I see him dressed as a pirate. A bird dressed as a pirate.

"We'll take you to your new school, Monday morning. Your father will or I will or *someone* will." Her face gets all tight-looking again. I hope that it's "someone" who takes me, not one of them. Then she says, "And you will *stay* at Connaught, Rex, if you know what's good for you."

Just then the Sausage starts howling. Why couldn't he have started up earlier? I should rig up some kind of electrical wire to my little brother so that whenever I need him to cry, I could give him a little shock. If I had a thing like that, I'd have got him to cry right about the time when Mum said "I'm the one who should be saying I'm sorry."

@ @ @

Dad gets home around four. He doesn't get really angry, but I can tell it's because his mind is elsewhere. I guess a bridge collapsing is more important than my life collapsing.

Dinner that night is quiet. Too quiet. Dad is too tired to tell any jokes. Mum doesn't ask if everybody had a good day, Letitia doesn't sing, Flora Bella doesn't put any food on her head, the Sausage doesn't cry because one of his carrots called him a baby.

And as for Annie Oakley: I don't tell on her playing hooky, but she is really mad at me for owning up to stealing the quarter before she got a chance to spill the beans. I stare back at her with the eyes of a timber wolf standing up to a mountain lion.

@ @ @

James phones just when *Twilight Zone* is starting, which would be bad most Wednesday nights, but is okay tonight because I'm not allowed to watch TV anyway. I tell him what happened.

"I guess it really was too good to be true," he says.

"Yeah, and it's not fair. Just because my parents like to

move all over the place whenever they feel like it, why should I have to? Why should I have to make new friends and try to learn about a whole new batch of teachers and what they want and don't want and figure out who I can borrow a pencil from and which is the kid you're not supposed to say anything about her mother because she just died in a car crash and learn which street might be dangerous because there's a big kid who lives under the bridge there and where the best candy store is and why that other kid's face is sort of saggy and where my locker is and which bathroom you can use at recess and where the nurse's office is when you get a cut playing football *if* anybody in the *stupid* school even plays football. Why?"

The other end of the line is quiet. I listen closer. "James, are you there?"

"I don't know why, Rex."

"I didn't think so. And I don't think it's fair that I can't stay where I am. Was. I can *get* to Hopewell, so why can't I *go* to Hopewell?"

There's another silence.

"James?"

"You've got me," he says.

◎ ◎ ◎

Kathy phones next. I tell her all the same things I said to James except now I add more things: "The teachers are used to me at Hopewell. They like me. Well, Mrs. Beauregard doesn't like me as much as she used to, but then she doesn't really like anyone."

"We're all lumps and bumps."

"I'm a good student. And the teachers at Connaught will hate me because now they've got one more person in the class, one more set of assignments to mark, one more report card to fill out."

"You should do something," says Kathy.

"Like what?"

"Complain. Kick up a fuss. Write a letter."

"A letter? To who?"

"The newspaper. The prime minister. Somebody."

"Maybe I could chain myself to the doors at Hopewell," I say.

"Or go on a hunger strike."

"Or kidnap someone's kid and demand to go to Hopewell if they want to see their kid alive again."

"I don't think that would work," says Kathy.

"I guess you're right." I don't say anything for a bit. Neither does Kathy. I can hear laughing in the background, her mom and her new dad, Dr. Arnold.

"I wouldn't really kidnap someone," I say.

"I know," she says. "You're just angry."

"Right. And anyway, it's more like I'm the one who's been kidnapped."

◎ ◎ ◎

Buster phones fifteen minutes later. And for the third time I go off on this big hairy conniption fit, although by now I'm kind of running out of steam.

"Yeah, I know," says. Buster. "James just told me all about it."

"So. Got any ideas?"

"Maybe you could run away," he says. I like Buster but sometimes he just doesn't get it.

"Thanks for the idea," I say.

"At least there's a good side to it."

"Like what?"

"Like Spew Lessieur said he was going to get you back for what you did to him this morning."

"What I did to *him*?"

"Yeah. He said he was going to smash your face into as many pieces as your piano."

"He said that?"

"Well, not exactly. He said he wanted to talk to you. But you know what that means."

A MIDNIGHT VISITOR

I stare out my window down into the empty darkness of our backyard. There's a little glint of moonlight on the fishpond, but mostly just a gang of shadows arguing over who gets to blow the bushes around.

Then I notice the light go off in the shed. I hadn't even noticed it was on. The door opens and a shadow steals into the garden. There's enough moonlight to know who it is. Annie, the mad scientist. What is she doing in there?

I hear Mum on the stairs, probably coming up to check to see if I'm asleep. I rush back to my bed, pull the covers over my head. I hear the door open. She doesn't come in, just stands there.

"Sweet dreams," she says. Then the door closes again.

◙ ◙ ◙

The inside of Connaught is a lot like Hopewell but darker, with cobwebs, and instead of electric lights there are those flaming torches hanging off the wall like in movie castles. Everyone in the hallway looks like Spew Lessieur with a few Puke-like guys and a few Dribbles thrown in. Everybody stares at me. There are more and more Spews, Pukes, and Dribbles, and soon they're banging into me, smashing me against the lockers, and the whole school is rocking back and forth like a ship out on the sea.

Way ahead in the flickering light, I think I see Kathy jumping up and down to get my attention. She's got a placard in her hand with my name on it.

"Do something!" she's yelling as she tries to fight her way to my side, but no matter how hard she tries she never gets any closer to me. Then she disappears.

Suddenly all the Spews, Pukes, and Dribbles move aside and there—standing at the end of his shadow—is this pirate with a peg leg and sixteen swords and knives and pistols and a parrot and a scar and a skull and crossbones on his bandanna.

"Aye! Thar she be," he growls. "The new cabin boy. We run a tight ship here, Rex Zero!"

Someone taps me on the arm. I swing around and it's Polly. Her green eyes look hurt.

"I thought you liked me," she says.

"Oh, I do," I say.

But she waves sadly and starts to fade.

"Don't go!" I shout. "Come back, Polly. Polly? Polly!"

She fades until there's just an outline and sad eyes floating in the air.

I feel a hand grab my shoulder—feel myself being swung around. I struggle.

"I won't go!" I shout. "I won't go!" Captain Partridge sneers and starts shaking me. "You can't make me," I shout.

"Rex!"

"You can't make me stay," I shout again. I want to hit him, but my arms are all tangled up.

"Shhhh!"

I thrash around, but I can't move. Then suddenly I can't breathe either, and I wake up with a hand pressed hard over my mouth. It's Annie. I can see her frizzy hair even in the dark. The moonlight makes her look like the Bride of Frankenstein. I stop thrashing and she moves her hand off my face, wiping it off on my bedclothes.

"Yuck," she whispers.

"What are you doing here?"

"I couldn't sleep, you were making such a racket."

I rub my eyes, look at my bedside clock. It's after midnight.

"What are you going to do?" she says.

"What do you mean?"

"About getting kicked out of school. You're not going to let them do that to you, are you?"

I rub my hands over my face. "Wait a second. You're saying I should stay at Hopewell?"

"You can't let anyone push you around."

I sniff—feel a sneeze coming on. I cover my face.

Achoo!

"Gesundheit," says Annie, and moves away from me down the bed. I sneeze again. And now she laughs.

"What's so funny?"

"It's probably me that's making you sneeze," she says. Then she gets up.

"I'd better go. Some of us have to get up for school in the morning."

She heads toward the door, opens it. A thin beam of night-light illuminates her face. "Are you going to be okay?" she whispers.

I sniff again and rub my nose. "Yeah. Thanks."

She doesn't move for a moment. Then she says, "Don't let anyone bully you around, Rex."

This is probably the weirdest thing Annie ever said to me, since she bullies me around all the time. She bullies everybody. But I'm too tired to get into it.

She leaves, silently. Then the door opens again and she pokes her head in.

"Who's Polly?" she asks.

THE CITIZEN CALLS

I wake up at ten-thirty. The house is dead quiet. It's like being home sick except I'm not sick. Whatever it was that started me sneezing last night isn't a cold.

Maybe Annie is right. Maybe I'm allergic to her?

My eyes are sticky with sleep. I rub them. I think about my dream. Think about Polly vanishing, her sad eyes.

I have to get back to Hopewell. That's all there is to it!

I kick off the covers. I've got to do something. Now.

There's a note on the kitchen table from Mum saying she's out.

The newspaper is lying open all over the table. I flip through it. There's a story about a boy named Michael McKenny who returned home after going missing for a day because his parents were too strict.

"I just wanted to think things out," he said.

There's a story about the winner of Steinberg's shopping spree, and another about three lion cubs being born at the Granby Zoo, and one about how people who eat bananas may not suffer heart attacks. There's a story about a girl who lost her pet turtle when she took it to school. If there are stories about losing pet turtles, why couldn't there be a story about me getting kicked out of school? Not kicked out of school because I did something bad but because my parents keep moving all the time. That's a way better story.

I've never thought about how stories get into the newspaper. I bet James would know, but he's in school, so I have to think it through myself.

Somebody has to tell the newspaper about me, I guess. But who and how?

I get the phone book and look up the *Citizen*: "Reader Sales & Service, Advertising, Newsroom, City Desk."

City Desk. That reminds me of *His Girl Friday* with Cary Grant and Rosalind Russell. Whenever one of them answered the phone they'd say "City Desk, Walter speaking," or "City Desk, Hildy speaking."

I rush back to the newspaper and find the story about the missing turtle. The article was written by Marty Peaslee.

I go back to the phone book. Can I do this? No. Yes! Anyway, what's the worst that can happen? A reporter laughs at me. Shouts at me. Big deal. Still, I sit staring at the phone like I'm waiting for it to ring, even though no one I know is going to phone me at this hour of the day. And no one from the newspaper is going to call, that's for sure.

An image of Polly floats into my brain. Not the dream

Polly, but the one who watched *The Nutty Professor* with me last Saturday, the one dressed in green plaid and velvet, who likes Maltesers. The one who figured out what my name adds up to.

I take a deep breath and pick up the phone.

"City Desk, Peaslee here."

I can't believe it. It's him.

"Hello? Anyone there?"

"Mr. Peaslee?"

"Speaking. What can I do for you?"

◎ ◎ ◎

Mum knocks on my bedroom door.

"Come in."

She enters, a shocked look on her face. "Two men are here," she says. "From the newspaper. They want to talk to you."

Then she gasps. I'm dressed in my best gray flannel pants and a clean white shirt. I want to make a good impression.

She combs the hair out of my eyes with her hand. "You knew they were coming?"

"Sure. I called them."

The men are sitting in the living room but they stand up when I arrive. One of them is skinny and wearing a skinny tie but no sports jacket. He's the one who jumps up first.

"Marty Peaslee," he says. "Pleased to meet you, Rex."

I shake his hand, which is sweaty. He smells of smoke and Brylcreem. His gravy-colored wavy hair glistens with Brylcreem and there's even a little gob of it dripping down his forehead. The other fellow should have borrowed some because his hair looks like a bird's nest, but he's got a friendly smile.

"Kev Atteberry," he says, shaking my hand. I don't really notice what he's wearing because all I can see is a big fat black and chrome camera hanging around his neck. The chrome glitters.

I look over at Mum sitting on the edge of her chair with her hands in her lap. I don't know where the Sausage is. Maybe she locked him in the basement.

"Have a seat, Rex," says Peaslee. And so I sit on the hassock and he sits back down on the sofa, while Atteberry fiddles with his flash attachment.

"Rex," says Peaslee, "I got the gist of the trouble you had over there at Hopewell School yesterday. Care to elaborate, say a few words about it?"

"Well, I got kicked out of school, like I told you. But it wasn't because I did anything wrong. Just that we moved and now I have to go to another school, even though I've been going to Hopewell since the first day of classes."

Peaslee nods and his eyes light up. He's pulled a little pad from his shirt pocket and he flips it open. "From what you told me, you were called to the office and—zip-zap—

you were told you couldn't go to Hopewell anymore because you were out of district. Is that so?"

"Yes. I guess."

"Now the principal there . . ." he flips the page . . . "Tibbitts. How was he about this?"

"He was okay."

"Didn't he scream at you, jump up and down? Didn't he give you a rough time?"

"Uh, not really."

"Except there weren't any ifs, ands, or buts about it, right? You were out of district and so 'Bye-bye, Rex Norton-Norton.' Have I got that right? N-O-R-T-O-N dash Norton?"

I gulp. Nod. He's got my name right but what happened at the principal's office all wrong.

"And what did you have to say to him about this expulsion, Rex?"

"Like I told you, I said it didn't seem fair. I think that's what I said. That's what I was thinking anyway."

"Good, good," says Peaslee, licking his pencil point. "Brave lad," he said, scribbling away. "What else?"

I'm worried now because I can't really remember the exact words.

"I think I said something about moving a lot and how I didn't mean to trick anyone, or anything. But since no one said I *couldn't* go to Hopewell and my transcripts—is that the word?"

He nods.

"Since my transcripts had been sent there from my last school, maybe I could just—you know—go there. Kind of pretend I was supposed to be there."

Flash.

Atteberry takes a picture. "Don't mind me," he says. My eyes see golden stars and I have to blink a couple of times.

Peaslee smiles away. "This is good. Anything else?"

"I told him—Mr. Tibbitts—about my friends and how they're the best friends I ever had, and how it wasn't fair if I had to leave as long as I was a good student and didn't cause any trouble and got to school on time."

"Your friends," he says. "Have you got their phone numbers?"

I hadn't thought about this. I don't want to drag them into this.

"Don't worry," says Peaslee. "Just want some background. I mean this is all about them, right?"

I look at Mum. She raises an eyebrow. Then I turn back to the reporter. What can I say? I give him their names and phone numbers.

He writes them down and then checks back through his notes. "And you are a good student, Rex?"

I gulp again, remembering the fight with Spew, but I nod anyway. "Pretty good. I never used to like school so much as I liked it there."

My voice catches and Peaslee looks up hopefully, as if maybe I'm going to start crying or something. And then there's a burst of light and Atteberry takes another picture.

"So you think you should be able to keep attending Hopewell, since you started there and all?"

I'm seeing double from the flash, but I nod. "I wish I could. I sure didn't mean to do anything wrong."

"Because you moved *after* your transcripts had already been sent from Mutchmor to Hopewell?"

I nod.

"Makes sense to me."

He flips back a page or two in his little notebook.

"You said you were pretending it was all right, so you must have known it wasn't *really* all right." Peaslee smiles and his teeth are crooked and yellow, like a crocodile's.

"I guess."

"And your folks didn't know a thing about it?"

"Well, yes. I mean no." I glance at Mum. Peaslee glances at Mum. She shakes her head, but she looks tense. Then suddenly Atteberry is on his knees right in front of my face.

"Say 'Bye-bye,' Rex."

Flash.

"And you were taking the bus every day clear across town."

"Two buses."

Flash.

"*Two* buses," says Peaslee, writing it down. Except now it looks as if there are two Peaslees. My head is spinning. "So it was costing you extra to go there."

I gulp again. Then Mum pipes up. "Luckily, Rex's allowance covered his travel costs."

I glance over at her, my face red, but she doesn't give me away.

"So here you are," says Peaslee, "willing to pay extra and get up early—because it's a heck of a hike, isn't it—and do the work and be an all-round great student, and they're chucking you out just because you're not in the district. Does that about sum it up?"

"I guess."

Flash.

"And did this Mr. Tibbs—"

"Mr. Tibbitts."

"Tibbitts. Did he say there was anything you could do about it?"

"Pardon me?"

"Can you appeal the decision?"

"What does that mean?"

"Can you petition the school board? Did he suggest that as an option?"

Petition the school board? Options? I never thought you could do anything like that. Then I remember what Kathy said about writing a letter. Maybe that's what she meant.

Flash.

"Any plans to take on the Powers That Be, Rex?" says Peaslee. "Buck the system? Take a stand?"

In my head, a vision of a sheriff pops up. He's going to

take on the hombres and clean up the town. Restore law and order to Dry Gulch.

"I'd like to go back to Hopewell. But I'm not sure how. I mean, what I want is to be allowed to go there without . . . you know . . ."

"Without having to *pretend* it's all right?"

"Yeah, I guess."

I know I was the one who said something about pretending earlier and I wish I hadn't, because when Peaslee says it, it sounds like something tricky. Dishonest. Which I guess it was.

"So," he says. "That about wraps it up. You got what you need, Kev?"

Kev is fiddling with a new lens.

"Maybe one more with this wide-angle, Marty."

"Any last words, Rex?" says Peaslee.

Last words. That's what the priest says to the guy on death row.

"I'm not a troublemaker," I say. "I didn't do this because I was looking for . . . you know."

"Attention?"

I nod. "I just want to go to school with my friends. And I don't think that's so bad, is it?"

"Not bad at all," says Peaslee, scribbling away. "Excellent!" Then he looks over at my mother. "Any words from you, ma'am?"

Mum frowns. "No," she says. "I think Rex has said quite enough."

"Do you and Mr. Norton-Norton plan on taking on the board?"

"I . . . I really don't know. We haven't discussed it. This has all been quite a surprise." She looks at me. "It does seem a shame. Rex was quite happy there." She looks down at her hands. "Then again, rules are rules. And sometimes things are . . . well, not the way one would like them to be."

She's looking at me when she says this. But Peaslee pipes right up. "Isn't that the truth," he says, getting to his feet and shoving his notepad in his pocket. "Sure is amazing you never picked up on it," he says to Mum. "Kid hightailing off across the city and you didn't have a clue that something was up?"

Mum's frown deepens, her eyes look angry.

"Do you have children, Mr. Peaslee?"

"No, ma'am."

"Well, I have quite a number of them *and* we just moved *and* there have been other upheavals in our life recently." Then she glances at me. "Besides, Rex has gone out of his way to keep this a secret from us. So no, I had no clue, as you put it."

"No need to get sore, ma'am. I just ask the questions."

"So I noticed," she says.

It doesn't even faze him. Peaslee claps me on the shoulder and gives me one of his crooked smiles.

"You're quite the little rebel, Rex. Good luck with this."

Rebel?

Flash.

A BIT OF TROUBLE

When Mum has seen Peaslee and Atteberry to the door, she comes back into the living room and sits down. I sit on the sofa and she sits in her wingback chair by the empty fire and neither of us says anything. I glance at her and she gives me a watery smile. Then she gets up and leaves the room and leaves behind a whole conversation that we never had.

I need some air. I figure I'd better tell Mum I'm going out, but when I go looking for her she's nowhere in the house. The Sausage is in his bed sleeping with his little piece of dirty blanket that he's had since he was a baby. He calls it Bongo. He names everything. And looking at him sleep it suddenly occurs to me that maybe he names everything because we call him the Sausage and he feels sorry for things that don't have proper names. Maybe I should start calling him Rupert. At least, I think that's his name.

I head downstairs and look out a window that overlooks the back garden. There's my mother, down by the stone wall looking out over the alley, smoking again.

So I just leave.

I don't know the name of the park at the bottom of the hill. It might be Sherwood Park because Sherwood is the big street there. Like Sherwood Forest where Robin Hood hung out with his merry men, annoying the Sheriff of Nottingham.

Am I a rebel? I don't think so. But maybe when Marty Peaslee writes my story, it will help get me back into Hopewell. Maybe the Board of Education will let me stay. Or maybe people will read the story and feel sorry for me. I'll become a cause.

Then again, maybe the board won't budge and I'll have to chain myself to the door of the school, like I told Kathy I was going to do. Except I doubt I will. It doesn't sound like a lot of fun. I've seen people do that on the six o'clock news, but they're usually fighting for something important, like liberty, not just wanting to go to this school or that one.

I think of what's going on down in Birmingham, Alabama. That's a real cause. My little problem seems pretty stupid and small by comparison. "A bit of trouble"—that's what Marty Peaslee called it. I remember his crocodile teeth and shudder. When I try to think of the interview I remember more of what *he* said than what I said. But what I remember most is stars in my eyes.

THE GREAT PRETENDER

T he story is in the Friday morning paper, on page five, the bottom right corner. There's a picture of me. My mouth is open like a fish and my nose is way too big, like when you look in the side of a kettle. The heading reads: "A Rebel with a Cause or The Great Pretender?"

I read the caption under the photograph first.

Twelve-year-old Rex Norton-Norton of 330 Fairmont Avenue will not return to Hopewell Avenue School, even though he's a top student, unless the Ottawa Board of Education is willing to heed his plea.

My plea? Who said anything about pleas?

I'm shivering and it's not just because it's seven o'clock on an overcast September morning and I'm standing in the front hallway in my pajamas with the door wide open.

I close it and take the paper into the living room. The

words swim in front of my eyes and my heart is pounding like a frog when you're holding it too tightly, and he thinks he's being swallowed by a snake.

I take a deep breath and start reading.

Summer doesn't officially end until 1:24 p.m. EST, Monday, but Ottawa boys and girls have already been in school for most of three weeks. School days, however, ended abruptly Wednesday morning for one excellent student when he was told he could no longer attend Hopewell Avenue School. Rex Norton-Norton graduated from Mutchmor Public School, and like most of his friends from the Glebe he looked forward to grade seven at Hopewell. Unfortunately, his family moved from the Glebe to the west end over the summer. Rex's transcript had already been sent to Hopewell and so he decided to follow the paperwork, you might say, even though it meant taking two buses each and every morning, and, more important, even though it meant keeping the whole thing a deep dark secret from not only the school, but his parents.

His friends were in on the covert operation. "They're the best friends in the whole world," said Rex at his home yesterday. Friends who have nicknamed their pal Rex Zero; friends close enough to be willing to break the rules themselves to keep Rex Zero's secret.

There weren't any ifs, ands, or buts about it, as far as Hopewell principal Marshall Tibbitts was concerned. Rex was out of the district, end of story. Tibbitts was phoned to corroborate this, but did not return your reporter's calls.

"It doesn't seem fair," Rex said, responding bravely to this harsh judgment. "I've never liked school so much," he said. "I don't mind getting up extra early to get there." When, dear reader, did you last hear a twelve-year-old say *that*?

"All I really want to do is go back," said Rex, on the verge of tears.

Petitioning the school board is a real possibility for this straight-A student. While there are no firm plans in place as of yet, Rex isn't about to go down without a fight. He's already shown that he's resourceful and plucky and ready to do whatever is required to take a stand.

There are noises drifting down the stairs, the ordinary noises of an ordinary day, but it isn't one bit ordinary. I stare at my stunned face on page five and it's as if I'm looking in a mirror.

Then Mum comes down and I don't know what to do. I shove the paper under the cushions on the sofa. She passes by the entrance to the living room without noticing me, on her way to the front door for the paper and the milk. She's back a minute later with the milk and no paper and this time she sees me. Her eyes look down and I follow her gaze and there's the newspaper hanging out the edge of the couch.

Mum leans against the wall and her head droops. I guess she can read the news on my face.

What is Mr. Tibbitts going to think when he reads this? I curl up in a ball as if someone hit me in the stomach. I want to hide. I want to go back to Vancouver. I want to go to the Amazon, cut my arm, jump in the river, and let the piranhas finish me off!

I fold the paper up as best I can because Dad is going to want to read it with his breakfast. Then I head up to my room, crawl into my bed, and pull the covers over my head.

There's a knock at my door.

"Go away!"

"It's me," says Annie.

"I didn't say half of that stuff. Marty Peaslee is a big fat liar."

"Let me in," she says in her something-is-up kind of voice.

I hurl my bedclothes off me and open the door.

"What?"

"Remember what I said about standing up to bullies?"

I nod.

"Well, that's what I'm going to do today."

"What do you mean?"

"There's a big football game at Fisher Park this afternoon and that's where it's going to happen, right in front of everybody."

"Football? You hate sports."

"Not *all* sports."

There is something wicked in her eyes, something that has nothing to do with first downs and field goals.

"Why are you telling me this?"

She shrugs. "Who knows? There might be something about it in tomorrow's papers."

I'm just about to ask what she means when the phone rings and Mum calls my name.

What now?

It's James.

"Why aren't you at school?" I ask him.

"It's five of," he says. "I'm calling from the phone booth across the street."

"Did you see the paper?"

"That's why I'm calling."

"James, I didn't say half of—"

"It didn't sound like you. But that's not why I'm calling. I just wanted to tell you that Spew Lessieur read the article."

"Spew Lessieur can read?"

"Let me finish. I can see him right now in the school yard with Puke and Dribble. They're laughing and looking at it. The newspaper. Just thought you'd better know."

"I don't get it."

"Think about it. Got to run. Talk to you later." And he hangs up.

It doesn't hit me until I'm halfway back up to my room. And when it does, I get all wobbly, like I'm going to fall over, and I have to grab the handrail really tight.

The picture in the newspaper and the caption under it: "Rex Norton-Norton of 330 Fairmont Avenue."

Uh-oh.

THE SECRET LAB

Why do they do that? Why do they print your address like that in the newspaper where anyone can read it and know exactly where you live? It's not just me, either. There's a picture of this really pretty telephone operator on page three. She saved a baby's life by giving the mother instructions in mouth-to-mouth resuscitation over the phone. The operator has thick wavy hair, sparkly eyes, and a lacy blouse. *Her* nose doesn't look big. *Her* face doesn't look stupid.

But that's not the point. Right underneath her picture, it says: "Judy Dallaire, 21, of 571 McLeod St., received a life-or-death call last night."

I bet she'll be getting a lot of life-or-death calls tonight, mostly from guys.

I get up and walk around in circles. Spirals, I guess, because eventually I end up at the front door, looking out the peephole at a gray fall day. No Spew. It's only ten in the morning. I don't think he'd skip school just to come and smash my face in. But who knows?

As if things aren't bad enough, Mum had to go out, probably to a smoking club to smoke her head off.

"Why can't you take Rupert with you?" I whined when she was getting ready to go. "What if he chokes or something?"

"If he chokes, call that operator," she said, putting on her coat and gloves.

"Where are you going?"

"Crazy," she said. Then she checked her purse. "I just hope I have enough spare change left to get there."

She gave me a good hard stare. Then she left, saying she'd be back by lunch *if* I was lucky.

"I might not be here when you get back," I called after her. "I might move to Pluto."

"Just make sure you take the Sausage," she said without even turning around.

At least the Sausage is in a good mood. Rupert, I mean. He's happy because I'm home. He wants to go out in the back garden and play catch.

"You can't catch," I say.

"I know," he says. "How about pretend catch?"

So we go out in the garden and play pretend catch. I keep looking up at the sky and hoping the clouds will bring a rainstorm so we can go in again.

I make some super pretend catches, which makes Rupert laugh. Then I pretend one of his throws is so hard it knocks me over. He loves that! So he does it again and again. And I just keep falling over. I'm pretty good at it. Rex Zero, the great pretender.

Soon he's laughing so hard he can't throw anymore, not even an imaginary ball. He sits down and in about three seconds he's found a couple of maple keys and the three of them are having a little talk.

I walk around the garden with my hands in my pockets. We could go in now, I guess, but there's nothing to do inside anyway, and why go in when my brother is having such a good time with his new friends.

I head over to the shed. "KEEP OUT—THIS MEANS YOU REX!" Hah! Big deal. I have no secrets anymore, so her threat doesn't mean anything.

I open the door and peer into the dimness. I reach inside to the switch on the wall and flip on the overhead light. I step inside looking for booby traps. It's ten degrees cooler and kind of stinky. I sniff and sneeze.

It smells strange. It just smelled like a shed before: lawn mower fumes, dust, mouse poop, and rot. Something tickles my nose. I hold it and look around.

The workbench under the window has been cleared and there are all kinds of jars and scales and little white saucers, glass swizzle sticks and one of those white bowls chemists smash stuff up in.

I look at the jars. There are dried plants in them. Some of the plants are whole. Some are crushed like the herbs Mum keeps in the kitchen.

I look around the rest of the shed and something catches my eye, poking out the top of the gunnysack in the darkest corner. It's a gas mask. I remember Annie bought it at the Ex a year ago. They were selling them really cheap as a kind of a joke because of the threat of a Russian missile attack. I wanted one, but Dad said they were rubbish.

When I pick it up, I see a Skippy peanut butter jar, with some ground-up plant in it. But what really catches my eye is the skull and crossbones on the lid, drawn with a grease pencil. Annie's not a very good artist, but I get the idea.

Poison. What could it be? Why is Annie making poison?

I think about what she said this morning. About dealing with bullies. Annie seems to run into more bullies than most people, but I have a feeling that half the time they aren't really bullies. You trip her by mistake and you're a bully. You ask her to pass the mustard and you're a bully. She seems to think the world is out to get her and she's not going to take it lying down.

But *poison*?

The big football game.

I remember the glint in her eye when she told me about it. I stare at the lid of the peanut butter jar. The skull smiles back at me.

REVENGE

um doesn't return before Rupert gets hungry, so I make us grilled cheese sandwiches. He says it's the best lunch he's ever had, but I think that's just because I let him play with his Dinky Toys at the table. There's a bit of a mess when his Rover spins out in the ketchup and somehow his Austin Healey ends up in the milk jug, but I clean up pretty well before Mum gets home. She apologizes that her appointment went so long and then puts Rupert down for his nap.

"He seems to have had a good time," she says when she comes downstairs again. "Maybe I'll just keep you at home for good."

She goes to the kitchen to put on the kettle. That's when I ask if I can go out.

"Where?" she asks suspiciously.

"I thought I'd better take another look at my new school," I say.

From the look on her face I can tell she's not sure what to think. But she lets me go, says she's going to take a cup of tea up to bed. Have a nap herself.

As I'm biking down Fairmont, I wonder why any grownup would want a nap in the middle of the day. And what did she mean by an "appointment"?

I head down to Connaught to remind myself of what it's like. When I came down here last, it was the school I *wasn't* going to go to.

It looks different now. And it looks different for another reason: there are actually students in it. Kind of like a shell when there's actually a snail in it. It's not like it's really going to move much of anywhere, but there's this feeling that it could.

I bike around the empty playground looking up at the windows where the lights are on and class is in session. I watch a girl stand to answer a question, a boy hand out papers, a teacher walk down the window aisle tapping her pointer in her hand.

It's like watching six television shows at the same time, except that nothing really happens. I look up at the roof to see where the guards are, the gun emplacements.

Another new school.

I might as well face it. The article in the *Citizen* isn't going to do me any good. Mr. Tibbitts isn't going to phone begging me to come back to Hopewell.

The clouds close in. It's like someone took a sponge

filled with gray wash and wiped it across the face of the school.

I wheel slowly out of the playground and head west on Gladstone, not ready to go home yet. That's when I remember what Annie said about the big football game at Fisher Park. I've tooled around the neighborhood enough to know where it is. I head over to Parkdale, south on Parkdale to Tyndall, and then across to Holland. I stop and watch a number six bus go by. I've never taken it this far. This is the last leg of its route before it heads back toward town.

My bus. Well, not anymore.

I guess it's a special sports day, because it's only two o'clock and school is out. I feel a little weird. I'm afraid someone is going to ask what I'm doing there. I'm afraid someone might recognize me from the article in the paper. I lean my bike against a fence and head toward the stands, which is where most of the kids are heading. The game is about to begin.

It doesn't take me long to realize that no one even sees me. I've become invisible. This is going to be my high school in a couple of years, I tell myself. And then I laugh. Yeah, right! By then we'll have moved to Timbuktu. I'll be registered at Timbuktu High.

Fisher Park is playing Nepean. Some of the away fans are there, dressed in blue and gold scarves or jackets. But most of the people in the stands are wearing something red. Not Annie. She's all in black. She waves at me from the top row of the bleachers almost as if she was expecting me. I make my way up to her and George.

George isn't wearing anything red either. She's in a white blouse and a pleated brown skirt, kneesocks and penny loafers with no pennies in them. Her jacket is draped over her shoulders. She's sitting with her arms crossed, looking like she'd rather be anywhere else.

She smiles shyly at me and moves to let me sit between them.

Annie is busy whistling and waving her hands around like a real fan. George frowns at her. She and I are the only ones here who know this act is all fake. Annie is pretty good at pretending, too.

"What's going on?" I whisper to George.

George squeezes herself a little tighter. Her hands rub slowly up and down her arms, nervously. "Ask your sister. It was her idea."

I tug on Annie's jacket, but she ignores me.

I look out at the field. We're at the fifty-yard line: the best seats in the house. The teams are lining up for the kickoff. Fisher is going to receive. The Nepean placekicker steadies the ball on its tee. Annie sits down as if she's tired out already, but her eyes are flashing with excitement.

"I went in your lab," I say.

"So?"

"So, what are you up to?"

"You'll see."

The referee's whistle blows. The game is on!

Fisher makes a good runback to about the thirty-five. The crowd stands up, cheering, except for George. She's leaning back against the railing, her head down, picking at a fingernail. She has a pained look on her face. People who hang around Annie for any length of time usually end up looking like this.

"Go team go!" shouts Annie, jumping up and down.

It's first down and Fisher comes out passing. It's a cross-pattern for a six-yard gain. More cheers. I stand up on the bench to see the field better, scanning the players as they head back into the huddle.

"Which one is it?" I say, grabbing Annie's arm.

"Which one who?" she says.

"I found the Skippy peanut butter jar. Who did you poison?"

"You'll see," she says, pulling her arm free. "Be patient."

So it's true. I turn to George. She must have heard what I said.

"This wasn't my idea," she says. "I just helped with the science."

Oh, perfect. "That means you're an accomplice."

"I know," she says. "But there's nothing I can do about it now."

Doesn't she know that an accomplice to a homicide gets fried just the same as the guy who pulls the trigger? Doesn't she watch any television?

The next play is a run—goes nowhere. The crowd groans. Annie plumps herself down on the bench looking bored. I turn to her, whisper in her ear.

"You cannot poison people," I say.

"Some people are so poisonous already, it won't make any difference."

"Be serious," I say.

"Oh, I'm serious."

I throw myself back against the railing, like George.

Annie laughs. Then she sticks her face right in mine.

"It's not a deadly dose," she whispers. "At least I don't think so." She glances at George, whose eyelashes flutter nervously.

Oh, no.

Fisher has to punt. I survey the team, looking for someone who looks groggy, someone clutching his gut, someone ready to stumble to his knees.

It's a towering punt. The Nepean receiver catches the ball and starts running upfield, but he's tackled right away. Hard. There's a mighty roar from the fans and the crowd leaps to its feet.

The Fisher cheerleaders run by us down to the Nepean twenty-yard line, as the offensive and defensive teams change. The cheerleaders are in red sweaters, with white Peter Pan collars and a big F on their chests, short white skirts, white socks, and red sneakers. They've got red and white streamers hanging from their left shoulders. Five of them line up like the Rockettes, waiting for two stragglers to catch up. "Come on, come on!" shouts a bossy girl in the middle. They go into a routine kicking their legs up high. The two stragglers are not doing so well.

"WE'VE GOT THE T-E-A-M,

THAT'S ON THE B-E-A-M."

The crowd joins in.

"WE'VE GOT THE TEAM THAT'S ON THE BEAM

THAT'S REALLY HIP TO THE JIVE,

SO COME ON TEAM, LET'S SKIN 'EM ALIVE!"

Everyone shouts and hollers, Annie louder than anyone. I tug on her arm again, until she glares at me.

"You could go to jail!" I say.

She yanks her arm away from me. I sit there in a daze, wondering how this day could get any worse: me in the paper this morning looking like a fat-nosed goof, my sister in the paper tomorrow, in handcuffs.

I think of that grinning skull on the top of the peanut butter jar.

"What did they do to her this time?" I say to George.

"What do you mean?" says George.

"Did someone bump into her in the cafeteria line or take the last chocolate milk?"

"I still don't understand," says George.

"Annie," I say. "You don't know her as well as I do. She takes everything personally—everyone rubs her the wrong way."

"Oh, no," says George. "You've got it all wrong."

"What do you mean?"

"She's not doing this for herself." I stare at her. She shrugs again, looks away. "It's for me. I'd have never dared do a thing. I don't know if it's right. But it's something, at least. Something . . ."

She doesn't go on. I don't know what to say. I turn my attention back to the game. Nepean runs a reverse and the speedy wide receiver comes charging up the field our way.

"STOP HIM! STOP HIM!"

A Fisher player makes a good open-field tackle and the two of them roll out of bounds, right below us. The crowd starts up a chant.

"DEE-FENSE. DEE-FENSE!"

Annie hits me on the arm. "Here they come," she says. She looks at George. "Here they come!"

The cheerleading squad is racing up the sideline to keep up with the action. They stop directly below us, jumping up and down, clapping.

"Hut, hut, hut!" shouts the Nepean quarterback and takes the snap. There is the bang and rattle and grunt as the offensive line smashes into the defensive line. The quarterback drops back to pass but he trips and falls, and before he can recover, a Fisher Park guy is on him, pinning him down. The whistle blows, the quarterback pushes the tackler off him and jumps to his feet. The tackler from the Redmen doesn't move.

I watch as his teammates gather around him. He looks

like a big, strong guy. I get a sinking feeling. Oh, no, this is it. It's the poison kicking in. Any moment he's going to start throwing up.

The trainers run out onto the field.

"Get up," I say to myself, my hands clasped in front of my face. "Please, get up!"

The crowd watches anxiously. The cheerleaders are ready to start up a new cheer.

Except for two of them. It's the two who straggled into the routine down the field, the two who didn't kick so high. One of them, with bubbly blond curls, is sneezing her head off. The one with short brown pigtails is squirming and scratching. The other cheerleaders look annoyed. The captain, her hands on her hips, yells and the Sneezer yells back.

Annie starts to clap loudly.

The Sneezer is really sneezing now and that's when it hits me. Annie coming to my room that night. Me sneezing. *It's probably me that's making you sneeze.* That's what she said.

Meanwhile, a couple of beefy linemen help the tackler to his feet and off the field. He's limping, must have turned his ankle or something, so he's not the one Annie poisoned.

It's the cheerleaders.

Pigtails is writhing like crazy now, grabbing at the back of her sweater like she wants to rip it off, while her other hand is raking her chest.

The blond sneezer is crying, her nose is red and running, but now she starts scratching, too—scratching and twisting like she's doing some weird new dance craze.

No one's watching the game anymore, not even the players, not even the ref. The two girls are bopping around as if they're being stung by a swarm of wasps. Their eyes are streaming. The other cheerleaders try to help but can't get near them.

People in the stands watch in stunned silence. A few people laugh.

"GO GIRLS GO! GO GIRLS GO!" some guy shouts.

Someone else cries out, "Get a doctor!"

This woman, a teacher I guess, goes over to the two girls and manages to lead them away by the arm down the sidelines. But they break away from her and run toward the school, their arms over their heads. Only when they're out of sight does anyone breathe again.

The ref blows his whistle for the game to resume.

"Let's go," says George.

"Yeah," says Annie. "That's about as much football as I can stand."

OKRA AND HELLEBORE

I'm not sure why I stay at the game after Annie and George leave. Partly it's because I'm stunned. Partly it's because I don't know what I would say to Annie right now. What did those cheerleaders do to George? And what did Annie do to them?

The rain doesn't come until the fourth quarter. Nepean is ahead by three touchdowns by then. The crowd thins out.

Finally, I head home, soaked clear through to the bone.

Fairmont Hill is too steep to ride up even in first gear, especially when your brain is in zero gear. I only make it about a third of the way up before I have to get off and push the bike.

I look at my wristwatch. It's almost five. Dad will be home soon and then we'll have dinner. At least there's that: a hot dinner to look forward to. And maybe, if I'm really good, I'll be able to watch some television tonight. I'm trying to remember what the Friday movie is on CJOH, when I get this odd feeling.

Some people talk about guardian angels. Some people talk about fairy godmothers. Well, I don't know about that, but sometimes I think I've got this faithful guard way up in a watchtower at the very top of my brain. And right now he's on the blower sending me an urgent message.

"Enemy at twelve o'clock, Rex," says the guard. I look up.

It's Spew, Puke, and Dribble.

They're in front of my place and they've already seen me. They're mounting up. I turn my bike around and wheel out into the street.

Honk!

A car swerves around me, spraying me with rainwater.

Then I jump in the saddle and I'm off. I throw the bike into third gear but the hill is so steep that pedaling is useless. I chance a quick look back over my shoulder—they're gaining on me, Spew in front with his black and gold varsity jacket flying out behind him like a cape. I wobble and almost wipe out on the slick pavement but get my balance back and try to think what's going to happen when I reach Sherwood Drive in about twenty seconds.

There's only one hope.

Right where Fairmont meets Sherwood, there's another street, Kenilworth, which comes in from the west.

It'll mean a sharp left at top speed on a wet road, but there's hardly any traffic on Kenilworth and it's all I can think of.

I feel like Steve McQueen on his motorbike with all the Nazis in the world on my tail. This is crazy! There's no way I can make a turn at this speed. But if I slow down too much they'll figure out what I'm planning. I could go straight through the stop sign at the bottom—the suicide option. But the faithful guard in my head, who is hanging on for dear life, shouts, "Rex! If that's the only other choice you've got, at least try the hard left. What have you got to lose?"

At the last second I pull over as far to the right as I can to give myself as much turning room as possible and then I lean left, touch the brakes as little as possible. I slide a bit, but get my balance back and *cut, cut, cut* toward the corner—cut hard—so hard my knee is about six inches off the road.

Made it!

I straighten up, stand, and pump like crazy.

Then from behind me I hear a howl, a screech of car brakes, and a crash.

I stop. Look back.

Dribble has gone right across the Sherwood intersection—clear through the rush-hour traffic—and is sailing out of view down Fairmont.

But Spew and Puke have crashed into a tree—a huge maple. The two of them are on the ground. Well, Spew is on the ground and Puke is sort of draped over him and the bikes. One of the bikes has a badly twisted front wheel.

Spew yells at Puke, punches him, pushes him off. I should leave, but my eyes are glued to the scene. Spew climbs out from under the wreckage. He's holding his arm. I wonder if it's broken. But it's really only his sleeve he's looking at. The golden arm of the jacket is torn.

He looks up, looks at me. I'm about fifty yards away but even from this distance I can see that his face looks shattered.

"You've done it now, Zero," he shouts. "You are dead! DEAD!"

I don't wait around to see what happens next.

The little guy in my brain is shaking his head. "My, my, my," he says. "This is not going to end up well."

I'm afraid he's right. If Spew was angry with me before, I can't even imagine how mad he is now.

I head up Gwynne and the thought of Spew's anger gives me the jolt of adrenaline I need to speed the whole way up without even going into first gear. I see his face in my mind. He looked mad, sure, but something else. He looked scared.

Dad's car is parked out back. I hoist my bike up the steps and into the yard. I lean my bike against the shed. The sign on the door of the shed meant to keep me out is soaked, the letters all running together.

Mum sends me upstairs to change, and when I come

down everyone is already at the table. I apologize and tell them what happened.

Dad nods.

"Saw them myself," he says. "Bloke built like a bulldog?"

"Yeah."

Mum puts a plate of lamb chops and mashed potatoes and peas in front of me. She puts a dollop of butter on my potatoes and pours some mint sauce on my peas. Nothing ever looked so good.

"I got home early," says Dad. "Those lads were hanging around yammering like a pack of hyenas at the end of the path. Asked them what they wanted and the big fellow told me they were friends of yours."

"They are not."

"That's what I thought," says Dad. " 'Funny,' I said to the big one. 'I wasn't under the impression Rex knew any hyenas.' "

"You said nothing of the sort," says Mum.

"Well, no," says Dad. "But I did tell the top dog to hop it or I'd have his guts for garters."

"He didn't listen to you. They were still there."

"Rex," says Dad, putting down his knife and fork. "They're *always* still there: the fatheads and the nincompoops and the hyenas."

"Bullies," says Annie, looking straight at me.

"Exactly," says Dad. "The world is full of 'em."

"And they come in all shapes and sizes," says Annie. "Right, Dad?"

"Right, Annie. Eventually they become city councilors and then you don't see them around so much."

Annie looks at me, daring me to say something. I zip up my lip to let her know that I'm not going to squeal. I've got my own problems.

⊚ ⊚ ⊚

Later, when I'm dressed for bed, I knock on Annie's door. She doesn't answer, but I go in anyway.

"Who said you could come in?" she says.

"My name is Rex. I'm your brother. I live here."

She almost smiles. She looks as tired as I feel.

"What did you do to them?" I ask.

"Taught them a lesson," says Annie.

"No, I mean how did you do it?"

She glares at me. Not so long ago that glare would have backed me right out of the room, but I don't even budge. She walks by me and closes her door.

"It was a concoction we came up with: ground-up rose hips, daisies, and okra—"

"Okra? Like in chicken gumbo soup?"

"Right. The enzymes in okra can cause a lot of irritation, even lesions—"

"Legions?"

"No, *lesions*—wounds."

"Holy mackerel."

"Itching powder, Rex. That's all. I put it on their cheerleader outfits. Well, also some sneezing powder: hot peppers and *Veratrum album*—that's white hellebore. The alkaloids in it are really something."

She doesn't sound cocky or anything. She sounds like a scientist.

"Itching powder," I say.

"Homemade itching powder."

"That's what was in the jar with the skull and cross-bones on it?"

"You bet," she says. "Not deadly, but a good lesson."

"What did they do?" I asked. "Those cheerleaders."

"They're bullies. You wouldn't believe how mean they are. Especially to George."

"Why?"

"Why is anyone mean? I don't know. Did you notice that George has a mustache?"

"It's not really a mustache. I mean there are some hairs, I guess."

"Exactly. Did you notice she scratches a bit?"

I think about her on the porch that first time we met, rubbing her arms, and the way she held herself at the football game. I nod.

"Well, she's got eczema. It's pretty bad when it flares up."

"What's eczema?"

"A kind of dermatitis—your skin flares up and looks pretty bad. They tease her about it all the time. That's what made me think of itching powder. Give them a taste of what it feels like. Then I just had to convince George it was the right thing to do."

"She didn't look too convinced."

"Something had to be done. Those girls make her feel as if she doesn't even belong here on earth. As if she shouldn't be alive—or at least that they shouldn't have to look at her."

I don't know why, but I wonder whether they might have said something like that to Annie, too.

"Will they stop, do you think?" I ask. "I mean, do they know who did that to them today? Do they know why?"

Annie lifts her bare feet up and sits cross-legged on her bed. "I tried to talk to them once," she says. "Suzie and Beth-Anne. George tried, too. She asked nicely if they'd just leave her alone. Said she'd try to stay out of their way. That just made things worse. So, I told them to leave George alone or they'd regret it. Then they started saying nasty stuff about us—about me and George, like we were going together. They wrote lies in the toilet stalls, that kind of thing. They'll know who's behind it, all right."

"Aren't you scared?"

"Me?" Annie laughs, but not very long and not very loud. Then she looks kind of thoughtful. "I'm mostly just tired. I really want this to stop. It's up to Suzie and Beth-Anne now."

I lean forward, rest my elbows on my knees and my head in my hands. I'm thinking about Spew. I'm wondering what it would take to get him to stop.

REX WHO?

Saturday I'm not allowed to see my friends. It's just what I expected—my worst fears. This week I can't see them, next week something comes up and they can't see me. Pretty soon it's "Rex who?"

"It's not fair."

Mum is doing the laundry.

"You're absolutely right," she says. "Why don't you fold these clothes?"

"That's not what I mean."

"Oh, I see. I thought you were saying that it was unfair that I had all this laundry to do and no one to help."

I try Dad. He's making another shelf in the bathroom. For an engineer, he's not a very good carpenter, but he makes lots of shelves. The house is full of them.

"Why is Mum so grouchy these days?"

"I wouldn't worry about it," says Dad.

"Only, I—"

"She's right as rain, Rex," he says, cutting me off. "Having some women's problems."

That makes me shut up pretty quick. I really don't want to talk about women's problems. It's *my* problems I want to talk about. Except, she sure doesn't look right as rain. And what does that mean, anyway?

I look at the stuff all crowded on the counter that's going to go on the new shelf: creams and cough syrup, pills and rubs.

"It's not fair."

"Yes, but is it level?"

He's talking about the new shelf. He's put a screw partly into one bracket and he's holding up the other end.

"Sure," I say.

He picks up the level and lays it on the shelf. There's a little window with a bubble in it and when the bubble is between these two markers it means that the surface is straight. You can't even see the bubble in this case. He frowns at me as if it's my fault. He doesn't say it but I know what he's thinking. My son, the great pretender.

◎ ◎ ◎

James phones around five. He ran into Spew.

"Spew was in the Glebe?"

"No, down near Hopewell."

I want to ask James why he was down there on a Saturday and then I realize he was probably going to the Mayfair to see some fabulous adventure movie.

"He was standing outside this place called the Little Blue Stick. He called me over. Said he wanted to tell me something. I said we were in a hurry, and he got really mad."

I want to ask James who we was, but I don't because I already know the worst: it's a we that doesn't include me.

"Did you go?"

"I kind of had to."

"Did he beat you up?"

"No. He said, 'Tell your former friend Zero he's dead meat.' "

"That's what he told me," I say. Then I tell James about what happened yesterday—the bike crash.

"Oh, okay," says James. "Now I get it. I asked him what he meant. And he said 'What part don't you get, Egghead?' So I said the former friend part, because we're still friends, right?"

I nod at the phone.

"Rex?"

"Yes," I say. "Of course we're still friends. Then what'd he say?"

"He said, 'I meant former because once he's dead he won't be your friend no more.' "

"Oh."

"I thought it was pretty funny."

"You what!"

"Okay, okay. Not really funny. I was just surprised that Spew would put it that way."

"That's he's going to kill me?"

"Not that. Oh, forget it. Anyway, just then this huge guy comes out of the Little Blue Stick. I think it must be his dad and he just reeks of booze."

"It's a tavern?"

"Right. And he comes up to Spew and throws his arm around his shoulder. He's so big, Spew kind of buckles."

I try to think of anything so big it would make Spew buckle. "So he was really drunk?"

"Plastered, but there's more. We watch them kind of stumble along the sidewalk and Spew opens the passenger door of this old rattletrap and kind of dumps his old man in."

"In the passenger side?"

"Right. And then what? What do you think happened next?"

"Are you telling me Spew drove the car?"

"Yep."

"Holy mackerel."

"Really, it's true."

"He's not sixteen, is he?"

"Not as far as I know. He's around our age or maybe a year older. But he was driving. We saw it. And all I can say is it's lucky the old man wasn't."

◎ ◎ ◎

Polly phones Sunday afternoon.

"Kathy told me what happened," she says. Her voice sounds kind of breathy and nervous, which is good because so am I. "She said you were trying to get the school board to change their minds."

"Well, I don't know about that," I say. "I mean, I'm not sure what to do."

"I saw the paper."

Just what I *didn't* want to hear. "I thought you were away."

"I was. But the papers were all stacked up on our porch when we got back and my mom noticed your name."

"She did? How?"

"Well, from when you asked me to your birthday party and from when we went to the movies. I kind of had to tell her all about you."

I imagine Polly talking about me to her mother. Then I remember the stupid article. "The reporter got a lot of things wrong," I say. "I hope your mother doesn't think I'm dumb."

"Oh, no," says Polly. "She's kind of radical. She teaches at the university."

I'm not sure what "radical" means but I get the idea that it's all right. "I just hoped maybe it would, you know, get the story out there."

"It was a good idea. My mother says it was very tactical."

Tactical? Like an army maneuver? For one whole second I feel like I did something clever, but then reality crashes back in.

"Yeah, well it didn't get me anywhere," I say.

"You have to be patient," says Polly. "That's what my mom says."

"I guess. But meanwhile I've got to go to school Monday."

"And it won't be Hopewell?"

"It won't be Hopewell."

"Oh," she says. And that word—the way she says it—seems like a huge treasure chest chockablock full of other words, but I don't have the key to open it.

"I won't like it," I say. "I'll hate it."

"Maybe it will be okay."

"It won't. It will be horrible."

I want to say "Because you won't be there," but I can't.

There's this pause as big as the Grand Canyon. I'm afraid she'll hang up, so I quickly try to think of something else to say—anything.

"How was Cleveland?"

"Fun," she says, relieved, I think. "I have cousins there."

"Do I say Happy New Year?" I ask.

She laughs. "You can if you want. Thanks."

Another pause. How do people do this? How do you talk to a girl on the phone?

"I guess I should go now," she says.

"Okay," I say. "Thanks for phoning." Except, really, I want to scream, *Don't go.*

"Good luck," she says. "Tomorrow, I mean."

"Thanks, I'll need it."

"Bye, Rex."

Now! *Now* I need to say something. What? Something about "I'll see you." Something about "I'll call." Something about "It just won't be the same without you."

"Bye, Polly," I say. Then I hang up.

I stand there in the hall happy and sad, angry and in seventh heaven—well, fifth heaven, maybe.

I should have asked her what twelve meant, numeronautically, or whatever the word was. I remember her spelling out my name and then toting up the numbers on her fingers as we walked home from the movie. Twelve—that's what I added up to. But what does that mean?

Then the phone rings again.

"Hello?"

"It's me again," says Polly. "I forgot to say that Kathy told me about what happened with Stewart Lessieur. About your project. Your piano."

"Oh, right."

"That's terrible. I'd have really liked to see it," she says. "The piano, I mean."

For one moment my little shiny piano is back. There it

is in my mind's eye again, perfect and gleaming, with music pouring out of it. Then it's crushed. Smashed. A bunch of balsa wood bones.

"Yeah, well . . ."

"Anyway, I'm sorry," she says.

"Me, too," I say. "Because I really wanted you to see it, too."

◎ ◎ ◎

I'm in the hall at Connaught, but this time it's empty. Only a few of the flaming torches lining the walls are lit, so there are lots of shadows. The floor is flagstone and every step I take echoes. I hear shouting somewhere. A scream. Horror-show laughter. Then I realize the footsteps I'm hearing aren't just my own. I turn around and Spew Lessieur is standing at the end of the hallway. He starts charging toward me like a football player. I turn to run but I can't move. My feet are rooted to the ground. "You're dead meat, Zero," he shouts. "DEAD MEAT!"

I wake up in a sweat with the words "dead meat" swirling around me. I lie there trying to get my breathing back. It's like he's still inside me, charging down the hall, getting nearer and nearer.

I'm not sure whose bicycle got wrecked in the crash at the bottom of Fairmont, but it doesn't really matter. He can drive! He's my age and he drives a car. What am I going to do? I can't just sit around waiting for him. Calm down, I tell myself. And after a while, I manage it. I look at my clock: just after midnight. But I don't feel one bit sleepy. Tomorrow's my first day at a new school, but there's no way I can sleep knowing Spew is there, waiting for me the moment I close my eyes.

Then it comes to me. A plan. Slowly, at first. Then, piece by piece, it fits together like a Spew-sized jigsaw puzzle.

I get up and check at the door. The house is sleeping, making its old house-creaking sounds. I grab my flashlight off the top of the bookcase, and I'm about to leave when I tiptoe back to my desk and tear a piece of paper out of one of my school notebooks.

Then I sneak downstairs to the bathroom, shut the door as quietly as I can, and turn on the light. It blinds me for a moment. I rub my eyes.

I turn to my dad's new shelf and look through the medicines. Dristan nasal spray. Perfect. I take it down and unscrew the pointy top—the part you stick in your nose when you're all blocked up. The squeezy plastic container is about half empty. I pour the contents down the sink. Then I screw up some toilet paper and dry the inside of the container really well. I do it a bunch of times to make sure it's completely dry.

I turn off the light and let my eyes get used to the dark before I open the bathroom door. No one is awake. I grab the piece of paper I tore out of my notebook and sneak down to the first floor and head for the back door.

It's cold outside. There's only a tiny hint of moon and the streetlights on Gwynne glinting between the trees. I switch on my flashlight and head toward the shed. The grass is wet on my bare feet. I should have grabbed some boots, put on a sweater or something, because pretty soon I'm shivering, but it's too late now. And it's now or never.

I keep my eyes peeled on the steps over the wall, half expecting a giant shadow to appear. Then I glance backward—sure I can hear him sneaking toward me. Nothing.

Sometimes I wish I didn't have any imagination at all!

I get to the shed, put the flashlight on the ground, and grab the door handle. It's going to make this awful sound. I lift it up with all my strength and slowly, slowly push.

As soon as it's open enough to slip in, I stop and turn toward the house. I'm expecting a light to come on, someone to appear at the back door. Nothing. I listen. No one. I slip inside.

I find the gunnysack, then I put my flashlight down in the wheelbarrow aimed up at me, while I put on the gas mask and adjust the straps so it's tight. It smells horrible and feels horrible. I hope this doesn't take long. I hope it works!

I put on the work gloves that are in the gunnysack. They're too big, but I haven't got a choice. I don't want to end up dancing around like a crazed cheerleader. Finally, when I'm ready, I dig out the jar with the skull and cross-bones on it. I pick up my flashlight and look at the contents. It looks like oregano or thyme or something you'd put in spaghetti. But it's dried rose hips and daisies and okra and—what did she call it? Hellebore. The name makes me shiver even more. It's ground as fine as dust. Good.

That's what I want—the really fine stuff.

I carry the jar over to the workbench, put down the flashlight. The lid is on tight, but I finally get it loose. Then I hold it as far from me as I can.

My feet are freezing on the wooden floor. My face is sweating inside the gas mask. It's hard to breathe. I unscrew the top.

Now I take off one of my work gloves and pull the Dristan container from my pajama pocket. I unscrew the nozzle and place the container on the workbench. My hand is shaking.

Scientists working with deadly formulas cannot afford to shake. But scientists working on deadly formulas usually don't work in their pajamas and bare feet in the middle of the night.

Now I take the piece of notepaper and roll it into a funnel. I stick the funnel in the end of the Dristan container. It's not a big hole; it takes a lot of time to get it right and I have to hold the funnel in place or the whole thing will tip over.

Ready.

I take a long deep breath and let it out to steady my nerves, just like spies do when they're setting the timer on a big bomb.

With one hand holding the funnel, I lift the jar and

knock some of the itching powder into the funnel. I have to shake it around, but that's okay because I'm shaking anyway—I can't stop.

Finally, it's done. I take out the funnel and look in the Dristan container. It's most of the way full.

I screw the long pointy nozzle back on. And holding it at arm's length, I squeeze the container, very, very gently. A little puff of the itching powder comes out.

I'm ready.

D-DAY

Monday, September 23, 1963. My own private D-day. Mum has left clothes out for me. She must have snuck in, like one of Santa's elves, while I was sleeping. I wonder if she noticed any wet footprints on the floor?

To my shock, it's not a tie, white shirt, flannels, and blazer lying on my bed. I guess she's finally realized that we don't live in England anymore and I'm not five years old. She's washed and ironed my favorite cords with the red turned-up cuffs and my favorite blue plaid shirt.

Dad is going to drive me. This is unheard of. Dad is taking me to school? Mum insists. I guess she's afraid I'll hop on a bus and go back to Hopewell. Kind of like those two dogs and the cat that found their way home through the forest and had all kinds of adventures on the way, except they didn't take the bus.

I climb in the car feeling weird. I can't remember ever

being in the front seat. I can't remember ever being in the car with just my father.

"Got everything you need?" he asks. I hold up my pencil case with the Indian beadwork on the side, and a lunch bag, in which I already know Mum has packed a Peter Paul Almond Joy as a special treat.

"Traveling light," says Dad, nodding. Then he gets his pipe stoked up and we head off. The car gradually fills up with smoke, until I start coughing and open my window a crack to let the smoke out. Dad doesn't seem to notice.

We park on a side street so we can take a gander at the playground.

"Is that big palooka from Saturday out there somewhere?"

"No, he was from my old school." When I say that, I get a lump in my throat. My old school where I went for only three weeks.

"What about that fella there?" says Dad. "The one in the black-and-white-check shirt, with the hair hanging down over his eyes?" He points at a boy leaning against the chain-link fence right beside the entrance. "He looks like a tough customer."

"He's wearing glasses."

"Oh, don't be fooled by that," says Dad. "The toughest private in my whole regiment wore spectacles. He used to beat people with them."

"With his spectacles?"

"No, of course not. He beat people with their own spectacles, but you didn't have to wear spectacles for him to beat you up."

"He'd beat people up with their own spectacles?"

"No, Rex, don't be silly. He'd beat people with a pair of knuckle-dusters he carried in his pocket. How could you beat someone with a pair of specs?"

"But you said—"

"The point is he was a tough customer *and* he wore glasses."

"Yes, sir."

"So what do you propose to do about him?"

"Who?"

"The tough customer. You might want to consider a preemptive strike."

"What's that?"

"Comes from the Old Norse word meaning to tie somebody's shoelaces together while he's combing his hair."

"Dad."

"It means taking care of trouble before trouble knows what hit him."

"Dad, I don't—"

"You know what I'd do?" he says. "I'd go right up to that chap there and poke him in the chest and say, 'Hey, you. I'm the new kid in town and if you value your hide you'll keep a wide berth of me. A jolly wide berth!' "

I look closely at my father to see if he's fooling. It's hard to tell. How can I tell him that I wouldn't say what he just said for sixty-four thousand dollars? Not only that, I never use the word "jolly" except when I'm talking about Santa Claus.

He smiles. "You're going to be all right, fellow-me-lad."

"I know."

"Your mother wants me to come in with you," he says.

It almost sounds like a threat. I haven't thought about it. Partly it would be good because Dad was a major in the British Royal Engineers and he's big and impressive-looking and sounds important, so nobody's going to give me any trouble. But on the other hand, he's big and impressive-looking and sounds important, so they might want to give me trouble later, when he's not around.

"Do you want to?" I ask.

"I'll come if you like," he says. But I can tell that he doesn't want to. And I don't think it's because he's in a hurry to get to work, either. I think he wants me to do things on my own.

"I'll be okay," I say. Heck, if there is one thing I'm used to, it's starting at a new school.

"I'll want a full report at seventeen hundred hours."

"Aye, aye, sir."

I watch him drive off and then I cross the road and enter the school yard. I look at the guy with the glasses slouching against the fence. I don't know why, but he straightens up and nods hello. I nod hello back. So far, so good. I cross the yard and a teacher by the door gives me directions to the office. Ten minutes later I'm sitting in front of the big brown desk of another principal—my second in five days.

We shake hands and then the national anthem comes on the speakers, so we have to stand, and I have a moment to size him up.

This principal sure didn't cut himself shaving. I'm not sure he shaved at all. And he didn't brush his hair very well, either. It looks as if something just flew out of it. It's sort of a gingery brown color and there's lots of it. His suit is sort of gingery brown, too. His waistcoat is ocher. His tie is the kind of brown that is called burnt umber and his shirt is buff-colored. I know the names of colors because of Paint by Numbers. If Mr. Partridge were a paint-by-numbers, he'd be every shade of brown. He doesn't look anything like a pirate.

"Well," he says, when we both sit down again. "I'm sure that the Misses Featherstone and Linkletter in the outer office have already welcomed you to Connaught, but let me extend my own welcome."

I nod, can't quite remember how to talk. It's funny how his voice is brown, too, and woolly-sounding.

"So," he says, looking down at what I guess are my transcripts on the desk. I can't see because there's a wall of books between us. The bookends are bronze gargoyles. "Are you the kind of lad about whom I'm going to be calling your parents every other day?"

Now I really don't know what to say. Then he holds up the Friday *Citizen*.

My shoulders fall. "No, sir."

He puts down the paper and plants his elbows on the desk. Then he plants his chin in his cupped hands and stares at me. One of the buttons on his shirt is undone. For someone who runs a tight ship, he looks pretty loose himself.

"Well, you don't look like a troublemaker," he says at last. "And Principal Tibbitts over at Hopewell assures me you're not."

"He's right, sir. The newspaper story isn't . . . Well, it wasn't like that."

Mr. Partridge nods. Then he moves the newspaper and looks down at his desk again. I strain to look over the wall of books. But one of the gargoyles gives me a dirty look so I just sit tight.

"Seems you're a whiz at art," he says. "Music. English. Yes?"

"Yes, sir. I mean, I like those subjects."

"What are your worst subjects, Rex?"

"Math and French?"

He flips some pages. "Did you take much French out at Pauline Johnson Public School?" he asks.

"No, sir. There aren't so many French people in Vancouver."

"Well, that explains your French. How do you explain your math marks?"

I shrug. I have no idea.

"Well, not to worry. Mrs. Linney isn't very good at

math, either." He laughs, then looks serious again. "She's your homeroom teacher. You'll have her for math, social studies, and English."

"Yes, sir."

"I think you'll enjoy Madame Desrocher, so your French will improve in leaps and bounds."

"Yes, sir." It sounds a bit like a command.

He looks up. "Art is Miss Braques, music is Mr. Gamble, phys ed is Mr. Metner. You'll meet them all, soon enough. A worthy bunch."

I swallow. A whole new batch of names to learn. He stands, looks me over.

"Well then. Shall we go and meet Mrs. Linney?"

THE CASE OF THE MISSING TARANTULA

Mrs. Linney wears pants! I've never seen a woman teacher wearing pants. They're black, pinstriped pants with a sharp crease, and a narrow shiny black belt and silver buckle. She's wearing a crisp white shirt and a crisp smile. The eyes behind her horn-rimmed glasses are smiling, too. Crisply.

"Rex, welcome," she says, shaking my hand with a good firm grip. "You're just in time."

Just in time for what? I glance at the class. Most of them are just looking me over, but one or two of them are smiling, as if they're about to have dinner and maybe it's me.

Mr. Partridge wishes me luck and takes his leave. While Mrs. Linney sees him to the door, I take another quick look at my new classmates. I don't see any dragons, any ogres. I look again at my new teacher. Her hair is chestnut brown and pulled back tightly in a ponytail. I've never had a teacher with a ponytail before, either.

She closes the door and shows me to my seat in the front row of aisle one. Then she takes her place at the front of the class and puts her hands together as if in prayer. Her fingers are long, the nails crimson, and she has many silver bangles on her wrist.

"We're writing a novel," she says. "What's it called again, Audrey?"

"The Case of the Missing Tarantula." Audrey sounds kind of bored, which is weird, considering the title.

"Yes. That's it," says Mrs. Linney.

"And we're going to make a million dollars," someone says.

"By Christmas," someone else adds. And everybody laughs.

"At least a million," says Mrs. Linney. "And share it equally."

"Does the new guy get an equal share?" This comes from a boy near the back. "I mean, we've already written the first two chapters."

"Well, that remains to be seen," says Mrs. Linney. Her voice is as crisp as her shirt. She turns to me. "Are you any good at novels, Rex?"

I shrug. "I like reading."

"Good. That's a start. I think you'll enjoy this."

It's not like any writing assignment I've ever had before. Everybody is supposed to write just one sentence, and then we're going to put them together somehow. It has to be one *good* sentence. Mrs. Linney doesn't want any boring sentences.

"Give me an example of a boring sentence, Mervin."

Mervin rolls his eyes, thinks for a moment, and then says: "The football team is good."

"Excellent!" says Mrs. Linney. "Totally boring. And why? Yes, Marjorie?"

"Because the verb is dull?"

"Lacking in action—precisely. So what would liven up Mervin's awful sentence, Larry?"

Larry scratches his head with his pencil. "How about 'The football team slaughtered Broadview.' "

A few guys cheer, people laugh.

"Brilliant. Now, can anyone give me an even more boring sentence than Mervin's?"

The girl right behind me shoots up her hand. "I can," she says.

"All right, Sherry. What's your boring sentence?"

" 'I can,' " says Sherry again. I get it right away, and look back at her to let her know. It takes a moment for others to get the joke.

" 'I can' could be a boring sentence, but it could also be a very strong one," says Mrs. Linney. "A simple declaration: I can. A sentence isn't necessarily boring because it's short. Why is a sentence boring, Sherry?"

"It's boring when the words aren't trying."

Mrs. Linney goes on to explain the rules for writing the

third chapter of *The Case of the Missing Tarantula*. Except that she doesn't do all the explaining—other people talk, too. They don't even have to put up their hands. I can hardly believe it.

Here are the rules: the sentence can't use any proper nouns; you can't use any "gutter language," as Mrs. Linney calls it; and you have to write the sentence in one line so that you can tear it up into bits when you're finished. Not just *any* bits. You have to tear it up into nouns and verbs and phrases and clauses.

Uh-oh, I think. I'm never sure which are phrases and which are clauses. But it isn't going to be a problem.

"We'll go over grammar in our proper grammar class," says Mrs. Linney. "All I want from you here is to break up your sentence into what seems to you to be its different parts."

So we all settle down to write our sentences, except I have no paper. I'm just about to ask Mrs. Linney, when Sherry pokes me in the shoulder and hands me a couple of pieces of hers. I blush and thank her. Then I try to concentrate and come up with an interesting sentence. I can't write "Sherry has beautiful sunset orange hair and pale blue eyes," because you can't use proper nouns and the verb "has" is pretty boring. So this is what I end up with:

The big palooka who smashed my piano crashed his bike into a tree.

After thinking about it a bit, I break it up into these bits:

1. The big palooka
2. who smashed my piano
3. crashed
4. his bike
5. into a tree

On her desk, Mrs. Linney has placed four boxes: the first says SUBJECT, the second says VERB, the third says OBJECT, and the last says MISCELLANEOUS.

I put "The big palooka" in the first box; "crashed" in the second box; "his bike" in the third box; and the other two bits in the miscellaneous box.

The rest of the class put their bits in the boxes. When everyone has finished, every student gets to choose a piece of paper from each of the boxes, if they like, or just some of the boxes. Mrs. Linney doesn't seem to mind. That's the sentence that goes into the story.

You can only look at the slip of paper after you choose it, and Mrs. Linney makes sure they're all jumbled up. I can't really see how this is going to make much sense.

A girl named Patty offers to write the sentences on the blackboard, so she chooses first:

Hockey tumbles at the sea.

Everyone laughs. Then a boy named Murray takes his turn and makes two miscellaneous choices. He wants to choose a third but Mrs. Linney gives him a look. This is what he chooses:

The enchanted girl until the people ran away sometimes slaughtered the village for him to catch.

Wow! And it goes on kind of like that. I find myself sitting on the edge of my seat waiting to hear the next sentence.

A girl named Penny chooses "The big palooka" for her sentence:

The big palooka danced in the Twilight Zone on his doorstep.

That gets a good laugh, and Mrs. Linney looks at me as if she is wondering whether part of the sentence is mine.

Once in a while a sentence sounds almost like poetry:

The ghost sometimes kissed the yellow silk dress of moonlight.

When it's Sherry's turn, she doesn't even pick from all the boxes because she likes what she gets from just the first two:

The orphan sparkled.

If we want to, we can write the whole chapter down. I do. And just as I'm finishing, the bell rings for recess. I thank Sherry for the paper.

"I'll pay you back," I say.

"Okay."

"Mark, Benji—show Rex where everything is," Mrs. Linney calls out over the clatter and squeaks and chatter.

As we head outside, Mark says, "Don't worry, it's not like this every day." And Benji says, "Yeah, sometimes we actually work." And all I'm thinking is, What happened in chapters one and two?

UNJUST DESSERT

I walk home worrying. I've got my Dristan dispenser in my hand. I've had it in my pocket all day, with the top all taped up so it doesn't accidentally go off. Every car that passes by, I check. Every figure in the distance is Spew. When I get to the hill at Sherwood, I walk over to Gwynne instead. Just in case. When I get in the house, I sit in the front window and watch the street. Waiting.

I phone James and it's kind of awkward, because I'm still kind of excited about Mrs. Linney's writing class, even though the rest of the day was pretty ordinary. I want to read him the chapter we wrote of *The Case of the Missing Tarantula*, but I don't want him to think I had a good time. So I say school is okay and the gym teacher is kind of tough and the science teacher talks funny. I tell him about some of the kids in my class and the weird smell in the basement, which is where the boys' washroom is.

And then I ask about how things are at Hopewell.

"Well, Puke's nose is broken, I think. Bruised pretty badly, anyway. And Dribble didn't show up at school at all."

I remember the last I saw of Dribble, gliding through the intersection at the bottom of Fairmont and right out of view. Maybe he really did end up in the river. Two more people who probably don't like me very much, assuming Dribble didn't drown.

"Oh, yeah, and Sami is moving back to Lebanon," says James.

"Really?"

"Uh-huh. Things could be worse, Rex. You could be moving to the Middle East."

"Yeah, well right now I feel as if I have."

"I'll really miss Sami," says James.

I already do, but I don't say it.

"Zoltan Kádár is this incredible cross-country runner and the captain of the cross-country team," says James. "Oh, yeah, and we're having a dance at Halloween. A dance, can you believe it? And . . . there was something else . . . Right! Miss Kisskiss sends her love."

I want to ask if anyone else sends their love, but I don't. By the time I get off the phone, I miss Hopewell so much it hurts.

Kathy phones a few minutes later. She's really excited about this petition that she started to get me back to Hopewell.

"You started a petition?"

"Yeah. I went around at recess and got people to sign it. I've got eight names so far."

Only eight?

"How's the new place?" she says, as if she doesn't want to say the name of my new school. As if she hates it for me.

When Buster phones, he only wants to talk about how stupid the movie was on Saturday.

"At the Mayfair?" I ask, although I already know.

"Yeah."

"Who went?"

"Just me and James. You should have come."

Right.

"Hey, are there any cute girls in your class?" he asks. I can almost see Sherry in my mind, but I don't tell Buster about her. He might tell Polly.

◎ ◎ ◎

Seventeen hundred hours is army talk for five o'clock, which is when Dad gets home from work and when he said he wanted to hear all about how my day went. But he's late and we don't really get around to it until dinnertime. Mostly I tell them about my homeroom teacher, Mrs. Linney.

"She wears trousers?" Mum asks. "What is the world coming to?"

"They're called pants," says Annie. "And I wish I could wear them to school. They're way better than a dress."

"Not better than this dress," says Flora Bella, standing on her chair and twirling so we can see it. It's cornflower blue with white trim and casserole stains down the front.

Mum frowns. "Sit down, young lady, and eat your dinner, instead of wearing it." But by then Flora Bella has made herself dizzy and topples right into Letitia's lap. She stays there eating Letitia's casserole instead, or at least the chicken parts of it. Letitia doesn't seem to mind. She's off in outer space somewhere, as far as I can tell, her head bobbing like a Sputnik full of music.

I tell them about the crazy book we're writing. *The Case of the Missing Tarantula.*

"What's a tranchula?" asks Rupert.

Mum frowns because she's trying to feed him.

"It's a *spider*," says Flora Bella, wiggling all of her fingers at him so that he starts to whimper.

"Oh, you two, stop it," says Mum, glaring at Flora Bella and me, as if I did anything!

But as soon as she returns her attention to Rupert, Flora Bella whispers to me loudly, "Is there really a tarantula missing? Is it in your classroom?" Now Rupert is squirming as if there's a missing tarantula in his pants—he won't eat a thing and Mum looks about as angry as a spider ready to leap on a fly.

Dad jumps in. "Since we're talking about bugs, I read in Win Mills' column the other day that bees are the only insect one is allowed to send by mail."

"Live bees?"

"Indeed."

"In an envelope?"

"In a box, I presume, or they wouldn't have much buzz left in them when they arrived, would they. Nine thousand of them at a time."

"Dad."

"It's true," says my father. "Except for the queen bees. They go first class, with just a few of their best-dressed attendants."

"Spiders aren't insects," says Annie.

"Nobody said they were," says Dad.

"You did so."

"He said bugs," I tell her. "And spiders are bugs."

Annie looks ready to argue but Letitia suddenly rejoins us as if she's missed half the conversation.

"And what else did you do in school today, Rex?" She sounds odd, like she's saying a line from a play.

So I tell them about how Madame Desrocher, the French teacher, is really old and she lived in Paris in the roaring twenties and knew some important painters.

"ROARRRR," says Flora Bella.

"Picasso?" says Letitia.

"No, thank you, dear," says Mum. "But I will have some more salad."

We all stare at Mum, but she's busy trying to spoon casserole into Rupert's mouth and doesn't notice. Dad puts his finger to his lips to stop us from bursting out laughing.

Mum's hearing has never been very good, but lately her temper is worse.

We clear the dishes and Mum brings in a bread pudding for dessert with a jug of steaming hot custard. We all make a big fuss—even Annie—and that seems to cheer her up a bit.

"I was talking to Dulcie Sutcliffe next door about the old country," says Mum, dishing some pudding into a bowl and pouring a drizzle of golden yellow custard over it. "It was she who reminded me of bread pudding—how she missed it, but never has enough bread in the house anymore to bother making it. Or anyone to make it for." Mum stops for a moment. "Lucky soul," she says, and then barrels on before anyone can comment. "Anyway, I decided to make some." She hands a bowl to me to pass along and while she has my attention, she says, "Rex, maybe you could take her a bowl a little later. I'm sure she'd like that."

"Do I have to?"

Mum glares at me and puts down the custard. "No. No, you don't have to do anything. Who cares about an old woman living next door on her own? I'm sure I don't." And then she gets up and leaves the room—*clump, clump, clump*—upstairs.

Flora Bella gasps. Letitia sighs. Rupert cries, "Mummy?"

"That's so ridiculous," says Annie, throwing down her spoon. And Dad just closes his eyes.

Luckily, the phone rings and Annie rushes to get it, even though we're not supposed to leave the table without asking first. When she comes back she glares at me.

"It's for you," she says.

"Can I answer it?"

Dad says, "I'm not sure if you can answer it but you *may* answer it."

The light is dim in the hall. I pick up the phone lying on the little telephone table.

"Hello?"

There is just breathing on the line.

"Who is it?"

I think the line is dead and then a low voice comes on.

"Zero," says the voice. "You are going to die."

THE OTHER SIDE OF VENGEANCE

Annie is in her room when I go up to bed. Her door is a little open, which is unusual, so I peek inside. She's sitting on her bed, looking sad. I'm not sure if I ever saw Annie look sad.

I knock. She tries to glare at me, but her batteries must be low.

I walk over and sit on the chair at her desk.

"What happened with the cheerleaders?" I ask.

"They weren't at school." She picks at the tufts on her bedspread. "But the head cheerleader came to see me. Connie."

"She did?"

"On account of the letter I shoved in her locker saying that what happened was only the beginning, unless Suzie and Beth-Anne stopped bullying George around. She said what I did was repulsive and I should be ashamed of myself. So I said, 'Fine, go tell the principal. I'm not afraid of you or him.' "

I look at her, amazed. "What'd she say?"

"She said they had talked—the cheerleaders, I mean, not the principal—and they promised not to ever talk to George or go anywhere near her."

"So it worked!"

She nods but now she looks almost ready to cry.

"What's wrong?"

She buries her face in her hands.

"Annie?"

She doesn't really cry, or at least her eyes are dry when she looks up, but I've never seen her look so hurt.

"George is really mad at me," she says, her voice kind of wobbly.

Now I'm confused. "But it worked, didn't it? Isn't that what she wanted—to get those girls off her back?"

Annie shrugs. Then her head droops again. She pulls out a whole clump of tufting and doesn't know what to do with it. She throws it on the floor.

"She says she wishes I had just butted out. She liked the idea of getting back at them until she saw what happened. It really scared her."

I can't remember when I've ever been on Annie's side about anything, but I am now.

"That stinks," I say.

"George says it got out of hand," says Annie loudly. "And it's my fault."

"But it's not your—"

"*She* didn't say it was my fault. She said it got out of hand. *I'm* the one who said it was my fault. And now she doesn't want to see me and I don't know what to do. What should I do, Rex?"

Annie Oakley just asked me for advice.

I feel as if this is an historic moment. Like when Dad and I are watching Winston Churchill's show on TV and he talks about a turning point in the war against the Nazis. I'm kind of tongue-tied. But she's looking at me as if she really means it.

"Did you try apologizing?" I say.

Her eyebrows come together, as if I've just said something in Chinese.

"Like, say I'm sorry?" she says. I nod. I half expect her to laugh out loud at such a ridiculous idea. But she looks as if she's thinking it over. Then her mouth turns down. "It won't work."

"Why not?"

"It would be a lie. I'm not sorry I did it. Only that it made her unhappy."

"So tell her that."

She looks at me as if maybe—just maybe—she's thinking about it.

"And don't yell at her when you say it, okay?"

She glares at me as if I'm stupid and I'm almost glad to see it because it reminds me it really is her. I get the feeling that now would be a good time to leave. I get up and I'm halfway across the room before she says something else.

"George said that I bullied her into doing this. She said being friends was enough. I didn't need to protect her. It was her problem and she would rather have handled it her own way, by herself."

She looks toward her desk. There are schoolbooks open there, homework to do. I don't know if that's what she's seeing. She's biting her lower lip pretty hard.

"That sounds hopeful," I say.

She looks at me quizzically. "Which part?"

"The part about friends being enough."

A PREEMPTIVE STRIKE

The thing about a new school is that you have no one to talk to about what's on your mind. Mark, the boy from my class, seems okay. The guy my dad spotted leaning against the fence with the glasses—the tough customer—his name is Aubrey, and he's okay, too. I show him my Whitey Ford and Sandy Koufax baseball cards because they pitched the first game of the World Series yesterday. So the next day he brings his collection of "Fight the Red Menace" cards. They're all about bad things the Russkies do to people and how America is ready to beat the pants off them.

"I've never seen these before," I say.

"They don't make them here," he says. "I just moved from Delaware."

"Wow. And they come with gum?"

He nods. Red Menace cards! Delaware must be amazing. We talk about who is going to win the World Series. I say the Yankees and he says the Dodgers.

But I don't know Aubrey or anyone else at Connaught well enough to tell them about a guy that lives across town who wants to kill me. It would probably sound like bragging. Whenever I think of Spew, I wrap my hand around the Dristan container in my pocket. I feel like I'm walking around with a grenade on me. It's crazy, but who knows where or when he might strike?

As I walk home alone past the park on Fairmont, I get this churning feeling inside. I stand at the bottom of the hill and look up. And all I can think is that I'm afraid to walk up my own street because of Spew. I take out my weapon. A Dristan nasal spray container filled with itching powder. Would it even work? If he came at me, would I be able to rip off the tape and spray it at him? And anyway, how much longer can I go around with this thing in my pocket? What if it opens by itself? What if someone bumps into me in the hall and suddenly this stuff is released into the air? Half the school might end up in the hospital.

I head over to Gwynne and I'm almost home when I stop again because something comes to mind—something my father said, the morning he drove me to school. A preemptive strike: getting your enemy when he doesn't expect it.

Yes.

Somehow I've got to get Spew off my back. It worked

with those cheerleaders, even if it's made things tough between Annie and George.

I think about that: about dragging my friends in on this. I've done that before. But this is different. If anything goes wrong, they would have to see Spew every day at school. So far it's only me he's after, but if they get involved, he'll be after them, too.

I take a deep breath. I'm going to have to figure out how to do this on my own. And soon.

Mum is sitting at the little phone table in the hall when I get home. She jumps up when she sees me and picks up something lying there. Letters. Two of them.

"For me?"

She nods. She looks kind of agitated. I never get any mail except from my grandparents for my birthday, if they remember.

I put my schoolbooks on the telephone table and look at the first envelope. The writing is in pencil, in a kid's writing. Lenny Argue, the return address says. I don't know any Lenny Argue. I open it up.

Dear Rex,
   I read about you in the newspaper. I hate school too. I bet your school is not as bad as my school. Good luck.

                                Your friend,
                                Lenny

What is this? Mum's standing there, so I hand it to her while I open the second letter. This one is in ballpoint pen and it's also from a kid, but older, by the look of the writing. It's a girl, I think. It sounds like a girl, anyway. Her name is Adiba Najib.

Dear Mr. Rex Norton-Norton,

Your article in the newspaper is not very mature. I hope when you are fourteen like I am you will be more mature. You do not know how lucky you are! Where I come from a lot of children do not even get the chance to go to school. I am thankful I can go to school in this fine country. You should be ashamed of yourself.

Yours sincerely,
Adiba Najib

I stand there shaking, wanting to scream.

"May I read it?" says Mum.

"Sure! It's as stupid as the other one." I hand her the letter and stomp into the kitchen, where Rupert is playing with Dinky Toy cars. I kick one so that it bounces off the stove. Rupert laughs his head off.

"Kick it again," he says.

So I *don't*. Instead I get out the Froot Loops and pour a huge bowl and a lot of it goes on the table. Then I go to pour some chocolate milk over it, except that there's only about a spoonful of it left.

"Aaaaaaarrrrrgggggghhhhhhh!"

That makes Rupert laugh some more and throw a Dinky Toy at my leg.

Mum comes in before I can do anything I'll regret, like dumping my bowl of moist Froot Loops on his head.

"I can see why you're angry," she says.

"Because those people are stupid," I say. "They both think I hate school and I never said that. Never! You were there. I never said I hated school."

She sits across from me, shaking her head. Then she leans wearily on the tabletop.

"You didn't say that," she says. "And even the reporter didn't say that. People don't always read the newspaper very accurately."

"I hate that stupid reporter."

"Please don't use the word 'hate,'" says Mum. "It's such an awful, unforgiving word."

"But I *do* hate him. So it's an accurate word to use!"

"It's just a couple of letters, Rex."

"No, it's not. You don't know what it is."

"Has there been trouble at school?"

But I don't want to talk. I don't want to try to explain about Spew's death threat so I push myself away from the table and head up to my room.

"Rex."

"Forget about it!" I yell.

I slam my bedroom door, twice. Then I lie down. My heart is bouncing around like an India rubber ball in my chest. It hurts. It actually hurts.

It's not the letters—not really. It's him—Stewart Lessieur. How can I get to him? Where? What am I supposed to do? Find out where he lives and then sneak in when he's sleeping?

I turn over. In my mind's eye, I can see that big old varsity jacket of his. If I could spray it with itching powder, maybe he'd get the message to leave me alone. He has to take it off sometime. Except I'm never going to be around when he does. Why? Oh, yes, I remember—because I live on the other side of the moon.

The rubber ball in my chest finally stops bouncing and just sits there feeling hard and worn out on this concrete floor inside my chest. I get up and head downstairs to get my books from the hall. I pick them up and find I've picked up a business card that was lying on the table. It's a doctor's appointment card.

Not our family doctor. There's a time written on the back, scratched out, and a new time written in underneath in my mother's handwriting.

An appointment.

I don't know what kind of a doctor it is, but I know someone who will. Kathy's mother is a nurse and her new dad is a doctor.

I peek in the kitchen. Mum's preparing supper. I run

upstairs and use the phone in their room. I sit on the edge of the bed and dial.

"Can you ask your mother what kind of doctor this is?" I say. Then I start to spell it out but she cuts me off.

"An obstetrician?" she says.

"Yeah, I guess that's it."

She laughs. "I don't have to ask my mother about that. She's seeing one herself. It's a baby doctor, Rex."

I WISH

There has to be some kind of mistake. I tell Kathy what my dad said about Mum having women's problems. But Kathy says if it was just women's problems she'd go to a gynecologist, not an obstetrician.

"But she's a million years old."

"No, she's not," says Kathy. "She's forty-three."

I don't know how she knows that when I'm not even sure how old my mother is.

"It's pretty old to have a baby," she says, "but it happens."

It happens.

"Is she still smoking? Because that's not good for the baby."

Oh, no! How much more can go wrong?

I don't say much at dinner. I watch Mum. She isn't fat yet—or is she? She's wearing one of her muumuus. They're this kind of loose dress from Hawaii that she usually only wears in the evening. But lately, now that I think of it, she wears muumuus a lot.

Pregnant. And just when we got rid of Cassie!

"What are you staring at, Rex?" she says.

"Nothing."

Rupert is being awful. He's throwing things. A Brussels sprout catches Flora Bella right in the eye and she starts crying. Then he flings a dollop of mashed potato on Letitia's blouse and she rushes upstairs to change because she has her big audition tonight.

"You are a very naughty child," she says as she goes.

"I am not a child," says Rupert. "I'm a sausage."

"ROOOAAARRRRR!" says Flora Bella.

How are we ever going to deal with another baby?

◎ ◎ ◎

By Wednesday, I've met all of my teachers. There's no one as wonderful as Mrs. Linney. And she's really only wonderful in English and social studies. We actually have to help *her* with our math. The other teachers are . . . well, teachers.

As for the kids, there are some I steer away from and some I steer toward. And then there's everybody else.

I go home, alone, but I go straight up Fairmont. Come on, Spew, I'm ready! But no one's there. So why do I feel he's watching everything I do?

At home there are three letters for me. I'm a bit more

prepared this time. The first two are okay. They just want to wish me luck. One of the guys goes to Hopewell, although I didn't know him, and he agrees with me that it's a good school. The third letter is kind of dumb, but funny. The kid wants to know if we could change places because he really liked Connaught but he moved somewhere else.

Annie gets home early. One look and I guess things are still not stitched up between her and George.

◎ ◎ ◎

I talk to James and Buster that night and tell them my plan about a preemptive strike. They're both at Buster's place and no one's home so they get on two extensions. I save the secret weapon for last.

"Whoa!" says Buster.

"But I've got to get a hold of some piece of his clothing."

"How about in phys ed?" says James.

"But Rex doesn't go to our school," says Buster.

"Thanks for reminding me."

"Yeah, but we could do it," says James.

"No way," says Buster. "Are you kidding?"

"He's right," I jump in. "This is my problem. I'll deal with it. But maybe you could help me think of how. It would pretty well have to be on the weekend."

I hear a click. It's James snapping his fingers.

"He plays hockey," says James.

"So what?" says Buster. "That's months away."

"No, he's really big-time into hockey. I think he plays all the time."

"Donnie Dangerfield!" says Buster. "He's our man. He plays hockey. I'll give him a call."

Twenty minutes later they call back.

"Donnie was great," says Buster. "He plays Pee Wee, himself, but he said Spew plays Midget with the fifteen-year-olds. Donnie knows a guy who plays with Spew. And here's the good news. Their next game is at the Coliseum, eight o'clock Saturday morning."

I can hardly believe it. "*This* Saturday morning?"

"That's what Donnie's friend said."

"You could spend Friday night at my place," says James. "Then we could all bike over first thing in the morning."

"Uh, thanks, James, but no."

"No?"

I'm not sure how to say this and not make it sound all wrong. Luckily, Buster says it for me. "It's a one-man job, right?"

"Right."

"Oh," says James.

"Believe me, I'd like you guys to be there," I say. "But—"

Buster jumps in. "Think about it, James. Like when the spy slips the drug into the bad guy's martini. You don't see *three* spies doing it. It'd be like the Three Stooges."

Sometimes Buster is brilliant.

"I guess you're right," says James. "But come over after?"

"Yeah. Thanks, guys."

As soon as I get off the phone, I get a piece of paper and write Spew a little note in dark and scary black letters. I fool around with it a bit until it sounds just right.

Not feeling so good? That's because I put a hex on you. And it won't go away until you stop threatening me. Got it?

Then I get an envelope, put the note inside, and write "Stewart Lessieur" on it. I'm not sure what I'll do with it.

I haven't talked to Polly since Sunday. I decide to phone her and dial really quickly before I chicken out. She sounds happy to hear from me and tells me about a party she wants to have for Sami and his brother Walli before they go back to Lebanon. She doesn't say it, but I think she'll invite me.

She asks me about Connaught and I decide to tell her about Mrs. Linney and about *The Case of the Missing Tarantula.*

"So it's working out okay, after all," she says.

"I guess. But I wish . . ."

"I know," she says.

THE TRESSOURVILLE TIMBERWOLF

I get to the Coliseum early. It's still dark and the air is as sparkling cold as ginger ale—even colder out back where I leave my bike, because there's a twelve-foot-high pile of snow back there. Man-made snow. In the shadows behind the Coliseum it smells like winter.

It's surprising how many people are in the lobby, considering how early it is and how the real hockey season hasn't even started yet. I reconnoiter the joint. Donnie Dangerfield told me where the locker rooms are. I'd sort of like to check them out, but the hallway leading there is narrow and I don't want to get trapped.

I hang out near enough to the front door to see Spew arrive, but next to a steel post I can duck behind.

The people in the lobby are drinking coffee in paper cups and eating doughnuts. There are a lot of beefy boys with canvas bags full of equipment and two or three sticks over their shoulders. Donnie explained to me that the game this morning is an exhibition match for boys trying out for the competitive Midget team.

I can smell those doughnuts from where I'm hiding and my mouth is watering. Then, finally, Spew arrives. He's wearing the varsity jacket. So far, so good. He's with his dad—has to be his dad—the one Spew drove home because he was so drunk.

He's not drunk now. He's swaggering. One hand is on Spew's neck. He's waving at folks with the other as he steers Spew toward the coffee bar. James was right. Mr. Lessieur's built like a bear. He's got big rolling shoulders and a belly that hangs out over his belt, but it looks hard. He sort of walks like a bear, too. He buys a coffee and starts jawing with some of the other fathers. He takes his hand off Spew's neck and Spew seems to stand taller, as if that hand was weighing him down.

His dad checks his watch and points toward the dressing room. Spew heads off lugging his equipment bag.

"Hey," his dad calls after him. "Knock 'em dead, kid. And that's an order."

A couple of men chuckle. Not Spew. He just gives this little nod and heads down the corridor to change. I notice which door he enters at the end of the hall.

Then I wait.

Mr. Lessieur is a real loudmouth. People don't seem to talk to him for very long, mostly just nod their heads and shift out of his range—careful-like, as if they're pretending they need to get another coffee or have to be somewhere else. After a while, he heads into the arena. As he opens the door I hear the echoey sound of a puck banged hard against the boards.

Spew comes out of the dressing room looking even taller and wider than before in all his padding. He's wearing a red sweater and leggings with black stripes and black hockey pants. He pounds the heel of his stick on the floor of the corridor as he walks. He's concentrating hard. I doubt he'd see me if I was standing right in front of him. I make sure I'm well hidden anyway, until he enters the arena.

I wait another minute in case he forgot something, then I can't wait any longer. I head down the corridor trying to walk big like I have a right to be there.

There are three or four other guys in the dressing room, tightening skates, wrapping black tape on hockey blades. I walk right on through to the bathroom, as if that's where I was heading. I peek out from time to time until one by one they leave and the place is empty.

There's a smell in the air like wet dog and something else, even worse. But I don't stop to think what that might be. Can't waste a second. Someone could arrive anytime. I dash over to Spew's jacket, lift it off the hook, my Dristan container ready. I'm wearing a pair of pink rubber washing-up gloves I found under the kitchen sink at home, but there's no way I could have smuggled a gas mask in here, so I'm just going to have to hold my breath.

I lay his jacket out open on the bench and spray the

collar as best I can. Then I carefully pick up each sleeve and spray a little into the armholes.

Finally, I grab the coat by its leather back and hang it up on the hook, just like it was, as near as I can remember. The whole thing takes less than forty seconds. I dash back into the bathroom and take a huge deep breath, leaning against the gray concrete-block wall. I'm shaking all over.

I throw the Dristan container into the garbage can beside the paper towel dispenser and push it way down, out of sight. I peel off the rubber gloves very carefully and get rid of them as well. Then I wash my hands.

The deed is done.

I head out into the dressing room again. Still empty. In the distance I hear cheering—the sound of a game in progress. I go over and look at the jacket again, but I don't get too close. In my mind's eye it's as if that thing is crawling with tiny insects.

The jacket is really old. There's a D on one arm and 21 on the other. I peer at the number. There is stitching there, and I wonder if that's where the jacket got ripped when Spew crashed at the bottom of Fairmont. The emblem on the front reads "Tressourville Timberwolves, 1947." It must have belonged to Spew's dad, which explains why it's so big.

I feel weird looking at it—weird all over. I wonder if maybe I inhaled some of the powder and my insides are going to start itching where I can't scratch. I panic—step away, still staring at the jacket. It seems to glow with danger as if those angry little insects are radioactive.

What have I done?

I head out into the lobby. I should just leave—get out of there. But I can hear the game, and without knowing why, I head toward the arena. I open the door and step inside.

It's colder here. I'm behind the net of the red goalie. Skating up at the blue line is Spew, number 21, like his dad. He's the left defenseman. His back is to me. I lean up against the boards, my nose almost touching the cold fencing behind the net. I make my way slowly around to the left, toward him.

Some big blue guy gets the puck at center-ice and starts toward this end. The goalie gets down in his stance and skates out to the edge of his box. Meanwhile, Spew skates toward Big Blue, meets him at the blue line, and—*Bang!*—rides the forward right into the boards.

I can hear his dad yelling up in the bleachers like a bull moose.

"That's the way! Kill him. That's my boy!"

Spew digs out the puck and passes it to a winger. Meanwhile Big Blue, number 17, gets up and skates back toward the action. Everyone is looking down the ice, so I'm the only one who sees him swat Spew hard across the back of his legs with his stick as he skates by. Spew buckles but doesn't fall. I lean against the boards, can't take my eyes off him. He skates up the ice, limping a bit, lifting his right leg to shake out the pain.

The blue team gets the puck again and heads down-ice toward us. The big right-winger takes a cross-ice pass and is racing toward Spew on a two-on-one. The other red defenseman is caught up-ice, so Spew is alone. He skates backward like crazy, measuring the distance between the two opponents, number 17 racing down the boards and number 27 not far behind him coming down the slot. Seventeen crosses the blue line, makes like he's going to pass it to 27, but keeps it. Spew isn't fooled—not for a second. He makes his move—quick as lightning—and drives the winger into the boards again, right where I'm standing. I jump back. There's just a four-foot-high wall between me and Spew, but he's too busy scrabbling for the puck with his stick to notice me. The blue guy is scrabbling, too. And swearing under his breath. Then his elbow flies up and catches Spew hard in the nose.

"Hey!" I shout.

I don't mean to. It just jumps right out of my mouth and Spew looks up, his nose bloody. There we are face-to-face, two feet apart. Our eyes lock and he looks confused as if he can't figure out what I'm doing there. Then *smash!* Number 17 plows him in the stomach with his fist.

I watch Spew's eyes bulge and his face get pale and then he folds in two and slides to the ice. Big Blue shoots the puck to number 27, who sails in, all alone, on net. He takes a wicked slap shot and scores over the red goalie's right shoulder.

The whistle blows.

Spew doesn't get up. The ref skates over to see what's up; so do a couple of Spew's teammates. I step back, kind of dizzy, as if Big Blue got me, as well. Now the coach has stepped out of the players' bench and is sliding down the ice in his shoes. Spew is doubled up. The ref clears people away.

"Give the kid some room," he says.

The coach gets on his knee, his hand on Spew's arm. He leans in close, talks to him, asks him something. Spew's head nods a bit and I see the stain of his blood on the ice. It's streaming out of his face.

The coach looks up. "Bring me a towel, Scotty," he says.

"Is he going to be okay?" a player asks.

"He's just winded," says the coach. "And he's got himself one helluva nosebleed." He gently rolls Spew over on his back and bends his knees.

Then out of nowhere, Spew's father appears. He's on the ice, too, bulling his way through the circle of hockey players. The coach sees him and gets up, moves out of his way.

"He should be okay, Frank," says the coach. Scotty arrives with a white towel, but waits with the coach as Frank Lessieur goes to his kid.

Frank reaches down, grabs Spew by the shoulders, and hauls him to his feet. Spew's face screws up in agony.

"Hey, Frank," says the coach. "Let him get his breath back."

But Frank isn't listening. He shakes Spew so that his head wobbles on his neck like a rag doll.

"What kind of crap was that?" screams Frank, in Spew's face. "You finish your check. How many times I gotta tell you!"

The other players skate away, but not the coach. "Easy, Frank. Jesus!"

But Frank hauls Spew up against the boards. "You call that defense?" he shouts in Spew's face. "You call that hockey?"

And then his big meaty hand gives Spew a backhand that makes his head jerk back, splattering blood so that I have to step out of its path.

Now the coach and Scotty and the ref and the linesman grab Frank Lessieur and drag him off. The coach is yelling for a security guard. Other parents are pressing in and poor Stewart just slides down the boards to the ice.

LAST CHANCE LESSIEUR

back away. People are crowding around. Two or three men are pushing Frank Lessieur away and the language is getting pretty ripe. A security guard comes and all the time Stew just lies there.

I slip out of the arena and then I run. Outside, the air is warming a bit, but not out back in the shadows by the man-made snow. I grab my bike; the handlebars are freezing. I want to get out of there as fast as I can. Get over to James's. No, back home to my family. My wonderful family.

I put my foot on the pedal and push off, but I'm wobbling too much to straddle the bike. I stop. I can't. I can't leave.

I rest the bike back against the wall. I'm shaking all over.

I can't let Stew put that jacket on.

It takes a minute for the truth to sink in. *I don't hate him enough.* Not after what I saw.

I head back into the arena, duck down the corridor to the dressing room. It's empty. I head over to the jacket, stare at it for one long moment, then carefully grab it by the middle of the back as far from the contaminated collar as possible, and start to fold it up.

"What are you doing?"

I turn very slowly. Stew Lessieur is standing there, a giant in his skates, his hair all mussed up and dried blood along the top of his lip.

"Are you stealing my jacket?"

I nod. "Yeah. You shouldn't wear it."

He takes a couple of steps toward me. I could probably run faster than him in his skates, but where would I go? The door behind him and the entrance to the bathroom—he's got them both covered like a good defenseman covering a two-on-one.

"It's contaminated," I say. "Your jacket."

"What?"

"I put poisonous stuff on it. Itching powder—really bad stuff."

His jaw drops open and his eyes crinkle up. "You did what?"

"I was scared of you! You threatened me," I shout. "So I decided to get you first." My voice is shaky, but I'm angry, too.

Suddenly, I realize I've got a weapon. I hold up the jacket by the arms like a shield in front of me. If he's going to kill me, I'm going to rub his face in itching powder first.

I'm not sure if he believes me, but he takes a step back. He closes his mouth. His eyes look more tired than angry.

"So why're you taking it?" he says.

"What?"

"You said you were stealing my jacket? Make up your mind, Rex."

Make up your mind, Rex. Good idea.

"I wanted to get you back for threatening me. But then when I saw what happened out there . . ."

I don't finish. And he just stares at me. He doesn't look like he's building up a head of steam. He just stares. Then he sort of smiles and taps himself on the chest with his fingers.

"Every time I get anywhere near you, trouble happens and I end up on my ass," he says. "My bike's broke. That stupid jacket's torn. I had a bruise on my rib cage for a week after you took me into the fence. Then you come here, yell at me, and I get sucker-punched."

"I wasn't yelling at you," I say. "That guy elbowed you. It was him I was yelling at."

Stew steps closer and I back up right into the bench. "If you come any closer, I'll rub this junk on your face and you'll see what it's like to be in pain."

He laughs and glances away. "You think I don't know?" he says.

He looks angry now, but I don't think he's angry with me. He looks almost ashamed—ashamed of everybody seeing his dad do that to him. I don't know if that's what he's really thinking, but it's what I think I see in his eyes. Maybe that's just how I'd feel if I were him. And maybe that's why I say what I say next, because it kind of surprises me when it pops out of my mouth.

"I'm sorry," I say.

"What'd you say?"

I swallow hard.

"You're sorry for me?" His voice is hard, as if I insulted him. "You think you're so special, don't you. You talk good. Show off in front of the class—everybody likes you. Well, I don't need your sympathy, okay?"

"Okay."

He looks like he's going to go on ranting, but then he just combs his hand through his mussed-up hair. "Put the coat back on the hook," he says.

"Okay, but I don't want you to pound me out."

"Okay, okay," he shouts.

"Ever."

"Jeez!" He folds his arms. "Just hang the coat up and get the hell outa my life."

I hang up the coat, carefully, with my eye on him the whole time. But I don't let go of it right away. Finally, he gets the idea and moves out of the way so I have a clear path to the door.

And that's when the door opens and Frank Lessieur steps inside.

"What the hell's keeping you?" he shouts. He doesn't even notice me and I slip away to the farthest corner of the locker room. I wait for him to move so I can beat it out of there.

"I thought they kicked you out of the building," says Stew.

Frank laughs. "Yeah, well they tried. Now get your gear and let's get out of this stupid joint." He catches a glimpse of me out of the corner of his eye. "What are you staring at?"

I can't speak.

"Aw, leave him alone. He's just a rink rat."

His dad points his thumb at the door. "Beat it, kid."

I head toward the door, taking the long way around, sticking close to the walls, staying as far from Frank Lessieur as I can. But he's not paying any attention to me anymore. What he's looking at is the jacket. His jacket.

"You won't be needing this anymore," he says to Stew.

I'm at the door, my hand on the handle.

"What do you mean?" says Stew. He looks my way—just a quick glance. But it's enough to make me stay, to turn and watch.

" 'Last Chance Lessieur,' " he says. "That's what they called me back in the day. *No* one got around Last Chance Lessieur."

He reaches out for the jacket.

"Don't touch it, Dad," says Stew.

His dad stares at him, like he can't believe his ears. "What'd you say?"

"I said don't touch the jacket."

Stew is standing as tall as he can, but he looks like all

his old man would have to do is blow on him and he'd collapse.

"No one tells me what to do," he says. "I gave you that jacket. Gave it 'cause I thought you were worthy of it. From what I seen out there, you're not worthy of nothing. You let that Sydlowski punk walk all over you."

"Yeah, I guess you're right, Dad." says Stew. And again he glances at me.

"You're damn right, I'm right," says Frank. And he grabs the jacket off the hook. He holds it out to look at the crest on the chest. "Last Chance Lessieur," he says proudly, swatting the crest with the back of his hand. "This is the jacket of a scrapper. A *real* hockey player. You hear me?"

"I hear you, Dad. Loud and clear."

"Don't give me any of your sass!" says Frank, and he starts to put the jacket on.

Something in me wants to warn him. But Stew glares at me.

"What are you doing here?" he says to me. "Didn't you hear my old man tell you to get out?"

Frank turns to look my way. He's put the jacket on but it doesn't really fit him anymore and he looks kind of ridiculous with his fat belly poking out. He nods his head at the door.

"Beat it, small change," he says.

"Yes, sir," I say. But I give Stew one last look. I'm not sure, but I think I see the ghost of a smile on his face.

MUM

What happened in there? Maybe Stew didn't believe me about the itching powder, but I think he did. He knew what he was doing. Instead of me getting my revenge on him, he was going to get his revenge on his father. I get this awful feeling in my gut as I bike home. I can't figure out why, at first, and then I realize. I'm frightened for Stewart Lessieur!

Pumping up the hill on Carling just before home, I feel the letter in my pocket, the letter to Stew. The edge of the envelope pokes my leg. I was going to leave it in the jacket pocket. Thank goodness I forgot.

I'm surprised to see Brian Odsburg's little Nash Rambler outside our house. He's Cassie's husband. Sometimes they come for dinner on Sunday, but they hardly ever just drop around.

When I go in, I know something is wrong. Everybody is

sitting in the living room. Flora Bella is sucking her thumb like a baby, sitting on Cassie's lap. Rupert is asleep with his head on Letitia's chest. Annie has her arms crossed and looks angry and scared. Brian is leaning against the hearth. He smiles at me sadly and waves when I come in the room. Mum and Dad aren't there.

"Where were you?" says Annie, as if they've been waiting for me.

"What's going on?"

"Mum had a miscarriage," says Cassie.

"What's that?" I ask, but I have a sinking feeling I already know.

"She was carrying a baby, but it didn't make it," says Letitia.

"She was pregnant," says Annie.

"I know."

"You did?" says Annie.

I look around the room. It seems that I'm the only one who knew.

"Is she going to be all right?" I ask.

Cassie nods. "Dad took her to the hospital just as a precaution. She should be fine."

"You'd think she'd have said something to somebody," says Annie. But she says it to me as if what she means is that I should have told her.

◉ ◉ ◉

They get home around three and we all cuddle around Mum and she gives us hugs, then goes off to bed for a good long rest. I go up to my room and lie down, exhausted.

Next thing I know it's five o'clock and the sun is sinking.

Downstairs, no one seems to be around except Brian, who is putting on his coat in the front hall.

"Is everything okay?"

"Seems like," he says. "Your mum is awake but decided to stay in bed, for now. Your father took her up a tray of tea and toast. Cassie is with Rupert and the others are off in their rooms trying to be quiet."

"Too quiet," I say.

"Makes for a change," says Brian. "I'm just heading to the Lucky Key to get Chinese takeout. Want to come, little brother?"

"Sure," I say. "Okay."

Brian gets lots of dishes with vegetables in them on account of him and Cassie being vegetarians, but he lets me help choose. I order sweet-and-sour spareribs and chicken balls.

Back home, everyone is downstairs again, bustling about without making too much noise, getting the table set. Mum is in her housecoat, sitting at her place, looking tired but more like herself than when she first got home. I go and give her another hug. And she hugs me back. Soon we're all sitting around the table opening the little red cardboard containers of Chinese food.

Everyone is starving, but we have to wait because Letitia has an announcement to make.

"I couldn't say anything earlier," she says, "because of . . . well, you know. I got a phone call this morning from the Orpheus Musical Theatre Society and I've got the lead in their production of *The Music Man* in November. I'm going to be Marian the librarian."

"Oh, no!" says Flora Bella.

"Pardon?" says Letitia.

"Are you leaving, too?"

Everyone looks perplexed, but I know how Flora Bella's mind works. "She's not *marrying* the librarian. Her name in the play is Marian."

"Oh," says Flora Bella with relief.

Everybody laughs and then claps for Letitia. Her glasses shine with happiness.

"A fellow Brian and I know at work was offered the part of Professor Harold Hill," says Cassie. "But he had to decline."

"Oh, too bad," says Letitia, but then her eyes brighten. "We're learning how to decline in Latin at school."

"Like declining a penalty in football?" I say.

"No," says Dad, "you decline nouns. Like Europe, for instance: Europe, Myope, Hisope, Herope, Theirope."

"No, that's the other thing, Dad," says Letitia. "The thing you do to verbs."

"Conjugate," says Dad.

"There'll be none of that around here," says Mum.

My older sisters giggle and Brian blushes.

"I don't get it," I say.

But Brian just hands me one of the cardboard boxes. "More chicken balls, Rex?" he says. He knows how to use chopsticks and shows me.

But when everyone is chatting again, I whisper to him. "I still want to know what the joke was."

He nods. "I'll tell you later." And I think he means it. It's kind of nice having an older person around here who might explain stuff to me.

Flora Bella suddenly remembers something and starts digging in the pocket of her cardigan. She pulls out a matchbox and opens it for Letitia to see.

"A tooth," says Letitia. "Congratulations." She hands the matchbox around the table and everybody oohs and ahs.

Flora Bella grins so we can see the gap in the corner of her mouth where it used to be.

"A canine," says Dad. "Well done. Canines are doing very well on the tooth-fairy stock exchange, these days."

"What's a tock exchange?" asks Rupert.

"It's an establishment where people lose their shirts," says Dad.

"Or make a fortune," says Brian.

"Do we get a choice?" asks Flora Bella, sounding a little worried. "Because I was just going to put it under my pillow."

"The perfect place for it," says Mum. "And make a wish."

"I will," says Flora Bella. "I wish—"

"Shhhh!" says Mum, but not angrily. Her finger is to her lips but her lips are smiling. There are dark circles under her eyes but somehow she looks like Mum again. "It has to be a secret wish," she says. Then she looks at each of us, one after the other—even Brian—and last of all at Dad.

And I get this nice feeling that maybe we were all once secret wishes she made, and she's happy she made them.

RABBITS AND HARES

I have a dream about my little piano, the one I made for music—the one Stewart Lessieur crushed. In my dream he shows up at my door and he's fixed it using glue and hockey tape. It doesn't look so good, but it plays. I play it for Polly. And when I wake up, it's October.

Tuesday, October 1, 1963.

"Rabbits and hares," I say to Mum when I come down Tuesday morning for breakfast.

"Rabbits and hares," says Mum. She's cooking scrambled eggs and wearing a dress that's the same color of yellow —scrambled-egg yellow, with little polka dots of white.

"Why do people say that on the first day of the month?"

"I have no idea," says Mum. "But I'm sure your father will have some ridiculous explanation."

She brings me eggs and toast and a glass of orange juice, and she scruffles my hair. She hasn't done that in weeks. I'll have to brush it again, but that's okay.

"Where's Rupe?" I say.

"Sleeping in. All the excitement around here has been hard on him."

She sits and has some eggs with me, just the two of us. That doesn't happen often, and I know it won't last because the others will be down any minute, so I make the best of it.

"Are you still going to smoke?" I ask.

"Heavens no," she says. "It was just the stress. Finding out I was pregnant. Such a silly habit."

"Which? Smoking or getting pregnant?"

She laughs. I'd forgotten how good a laugh she has.

"I'm sorry," I say.

"About the baby?"

That wasn't what I was thinking, but I guess I'm sorry about that, too. "No, I meant about lying and all that. Pretending I was going to Connaught. Not wanting to move and making things hard."

"Oh, Rex," she says. "If you only knew."

"If I only knew what? Is there something else?"

"No," she says, shaking her head. "Well, there's always something else, isn't there. But there are no more secrets. I promise." She pushes her scrambled egg around on the plate. "I should have let you all know what was going on. In a way, I was pretending, as well. Pretending everything was okay when it wasn't."

"But it's okay now?"

She smiles. "It's okay now."

EPILOGUE

We still exist! We being James, Buster, Kathy, and me. And Polly, too. The party she wanted to throw for Sami and Walli is going to happen and I'm invited. And as for the Halloween Dance at Hopewell? James is going to see if I can come. "We all want you there," he says. We.

But "we" is also going to be some new kids, too. Mark and Aubrey from my new school. We is up in the air right now, if you know what I mean.

"Well, the thing about it," says Dad, "is that, despite its name, which sounds small enough, 'we' is actually a very big place." We're sitting reading the newspaper together, just before dinner. I've got the interesting pages with the funnies and the puzzles and he's got the ones at the front.

"What do you mean?"

"There's a lot of room in 'we.' I mean, you have these

people in it and then suddenly you have these other people in it and there's room for everyone. Take our family, for instance. Once the 'we' of our family was your mother, Cassie, and I. Now look at it."

I nod. Then I think about the new little person who didn't quite make it into our family. It would have been a tight fit, but Dad's right. There would have been enough room.

◎ ◎ ◎

I find out we've signed a three-year lease on our house, so we're going to be here at least that long. Another good thing is that Annie and George are friends again. George comes over sometimes. One day, I told them what happened when I tried to get revenge on Stewart Lessieur using the itching powder.

James heard the end of the story from Stewart, at school. Apparently, his dad had to go to the emergency room at the hospital and get some special ointment. The jacket had to be incinerated. Just as well. I think that jacket was bad luck.

But that wasn't all. Stew told James he was spending more time at his aunt's place. She was the one who sewed up the tear in the jacket sleeve—the tear he got when he crashed his bike chasing me. Anyway, when things get rough with his dad now, he goes over there. So that's a good change, isn't it? I've noticed Stew's name comes up quite a bit lately when I'm talking to James and Buster. They went to see him play one time. They said I should go with them. I guess Dad was right. We is a really big place.